Unmasked

Joe Brink Mystery Book 7

tales from the pandemic

Phil Bookman

This is a work of fiction. Names, characters, places, conversations, and incidents are products of the author's imagination or are used fictitiously and are not to be construed as real.

Copyright © 2022 by Philip Bookman

All rights reserved. No part of this book may be reproduced or transmitted in any form or by any means, electronic or mechanical, including photocopying, recording or by any information storage and retrieval system, without written permission in writing from the author, except for the inclusion of brief quotations in a review.

ISBN: 9798840860465

Printed in the United States of America

First edition 2022

The Prologue of *Retirement Plan* first appeared as the Epilogue of *Sweetwater* by Phil Bookman.
Chapter 3 of *Retirement Plan* originally appeared as Chapter 20 of Sweetwater by Phil Bookman.

In memory of Ron Oremland

*"It's in literature that true life can be found.
It's under the mask of fiction that
you can tell the truth."*
Gao Xingjian

Table of Contents

Life Is Never Easy 5
Retirement Plan 89
Unmasked 147

Life Is Never Easy

Chapter 1

"That was no thunder, Joe," Boomer said. "It was my place blowing up. A real ka-boomer." He chortled with delight at his wit. I wondered how long he had been waiting to use that line on me.

"I thought it was another dry thunderstorm last night," I said. Which it was, and I'd heard a lot of thunderous booms in the wee hours.

"That's what they forecast," Boomer said, "but it never amounted to much. No, what woke you was my little chemistry set exploding when the fire hit the barn."

The massive wildfire dubbed the CZU Lightning Complex Fire had been triggered by thousands of lightning strikes and swirling winds from a freak tropical storm that had wandered way north of the East Pacific hurricane corridor, coupled with extreme dry conditions from a prolonged drought and an extended summer heatwave of triple-digit temperatures. It had already burned 80,000 acres, much of it in the rugged Santa Cruz Mountains a few miles southwest of my hometown, including, it would seem, the heavily forested peak where Boomer's cabin used to be. And the fire was still only about 10% contained.

It was my first day back at Brink Investigations, my one-man office in historic downtown Campbell, California, in the heart of Silicon Valley, after having worked from home since the pandemic lockdown began earlier in the year. I still wasn't seeing clients in person quite yet, but it was good for my mental health just to get out of my condo and be at work.

I was on a Zoom call with my friends Boomer and Sarge. The geezers were 50 miles north, onboard the superyacht *Sweetwater* that was docked at the marina in San Francisco. They had been living there since just before the pandemic and had not been back to Boomer's mountaintop cabin since.

Edgar "Boomer" Montana got his nickname as a young man, blowing things up for the U.S. Army in Viet Nam. He had since made a career as an explosives expert, and I knew he kept a lot of dangerous chemicals he referred to as his "chemistry set" in his barn for what he equally euphemistically called his "science experiments." Boomer had assured me more than once that he would clean up and secure the stash, particularly after the devastating California wildfires in 2018, but he apparently had not gotten around to that before he and his buddy Sarge moved onboard *Sweetwater*.

"How do you know that?" I asked. "It was loud, but

not that loud, and I'm about 10 miles from your property as the crow flies. Don't tell me you heard it from 60 miles away."

"I can barely hear Sarge snoring anymore, and he could wake the dead," Boomer said. "No, Joe, I heard it from Piscatelli."

I told myself to be patient, I had to let Boomer get to the point his own way. Besides, it wasn't like I was burdened by work and in a time crunch. There wasn't much call for a private investigator during our COVID-19 semi-sort-of-lockdown. "Okay, Boomer. Who is Piscatelli?"

"Massimo Piscatelli. Owns Piscatelli Vineyards just down the road from my place. Called this morning. Had to evacuate in a big hurry last night when the fire reached his land and was heading towards his house. Probably lost everything."

"That's awful. But what about the explosion?"

"Right. He said it went off as he was escaping in his truck. He saw it blow, said it was impressive."

Boomer went quiet, apparently overcome by pride at the pyrotechnics he had caused. Maybe wishing there had been a larger audience. I took advantage of the lull to bring the third man on our call into the conversation. "How are you doing, Sarge?" Also a Viet Nam vet, Stan "Sarge" Zampisi had fractured his skull during the *Sweetwater* Showdown.

"I'm okay, Joe. Just had a checkup and they tell me

my head's all healed." It was his turn to chuckle. "I almost said good as new, but that hasn't been true for a long time."

Never loquacious, Sarge had gotten even more reserved with each passing year. For him, those two sentences amounted to quite a speech.

"Good to hear," I said. "And no lingering effects from the virus?" Like Boomer, Sarge was deep into his 70s. He also had several chronic medical conditions that made him particularly vulnerable to the effects of COVID-19, which he and Boomer had discovered they had when they tested positive at the hospital in the aftermath of the *Sweetwater* Showdown.

"Nope. Guess I dodged a bullet there. But I think it sorta messed Boomer up."

Boomer chimed in as if Sarge and I hadn't said a word to each other. "Reason I called, Joe, is Piscatelli is gonna call you. He knew that I knew a PI and he needs one. I told him you were okay, gave him your number."

"Thanks for the powerful endorsement. Did he say why?"

"Nah, I think Piscatelli takes the private part of private detective seriously."

Chapter 2

About the *Sweetwater* Showdown.

It had started innocently enough when my friend Nick Marchetti purchased the superyacht *Sweetwater* for his company, Global Lunar Electrical Energy, where Nick, a Silicon Valley financial guru, was CFO. The plan was to electrify all of *Sweetwater's* systems and have it cruise the globe, demonstrating the electric-powered world Nick and GLEE CEO Mike Gold foresaw.

Nick hired Boomer and Sarge as live-in caretakers for *Sweetwater*. Then came COVID and the electrification project stalled. But the old guys kept their jobs and stayed onboard the yacht.

Just about the time Nick was buying *Sweetwater*, my friend Sally Rocket visited her sister, a fugitive murderer who was hiding out in the Dominican Republic. A paranoid San Francisco-based drug kingpin named Rick Varga somehow weaved Sally's Caribbean trip and Nick's yacht purchase, along with my past involvement in the capture and incarceration of two of his nephews, into the outlandish belief that Nick and I were making a move to take over Varga's drug smuggling territory.

Varga's delusion ended with what the news media dubbed the *Sweetwater* Showdown, when he and two of his thugs attempted to drown Boomer, Sarge, and me in the frigid Pacific Ocean just west of the Golden Gate. We managed to escape from our captors and survive. Varga drowned. And I shot and killed one of those thugs.

That all came down six months ago.

But it seemed longer, what with the pandemic, presidential campaign, and now the wildfires ravaging the state. Some government help and an understanding landlord had kept me afloat as PI work dried up, but now I was back in business thanks to those fires.

* * *

The insurance company employed its own claim investigators and used PIs like me for overflow work. I also got cases from them that, for one reason or another, they decided were suited to my special talents, though exactly what those talents were had never been made clear to me. In any case, they had had nothing for me since COVID hit.

But overflow was the operative word. When there's a major disaster like a hurricane or wildfire, the company brought in adjusters and investigators from all over the country to deal with the flood of claims. The problem was, there were a couple of dozen huge fires burning up and down the West Coast and hurricane season had gotten off to a fast start in the Atlantic. Even mobilizing all-hands-on-deck, there simply were not enough hands.

Which is where I came in. A few days ago, they sent me a list of properties they insured in the CZU Lightning Complex burn zone. What they wanted were photos showing the extent of the damage for each property. From those photos they would decide which properties were worth a more detailed site investigation by one of their employees. The rest, the ones where the extent of damage was obvious, they would adjust with their clients by exchanging paperwork.

The CZU Lightning Complex Fire wasn't close to being contained, and we would not have access for probably another week, if not longer. But they wanted me ready to roll as soon as the gun was fired.

Like a lot of my work, this was not exactly exciting. But the insurance company paid its bills. Which helped me pay mine.

Besides, I wasn't planning to do the work myself. Because, thanks to COVID I now had an apprentice.

* * *

I had a fancy camera to use for this kind of work, paid

for by the insurance company. Ricky Clancy was right on time to pick it up.

Ricky had been eking out a living in high-cost Silicon Valley driving for Uber and Lyft, supplemented with occasional gofer work for lawyer Ed Wax and me. Ricky took to delivering food takeout orders and doing package delivery during the pandemic, but that experience—earning barely over minimum wage and dealing with difficult customers—had finally tipped the scales. Ricky and I had cooked up a plan for him to become my intern and pursue his PI license. He was starting to take the necessary community college coursework online and would start accumulating investigative experience. Working for me. Brink Investigations now had a staff of two.

Remote work was the in thing during the pandemic out of necessity. Which was a good thing, because my office had just about enough room for me to operate. The good news was that Ricky was just fine working out of his apartment and his car most of the time.

I gave Ricky a quick camera tutorial and sent him home to practice. I also told him about the Piscatelli case.

Joe Brink, employer. Talk about adulting...

Chapter 3

Massimo Piscatelli looked like he had just gone through hell, which seemed appropriate having lost his home and business to a raging inferno.

He called me shortly after I ended the call with Boomer and Sarge, and we immediately switched to Zoom on our computers. Then went through some fumbling at his end. I went into tech support mode, and we finally got it all working.

We got through introductions, and I expressed my regret to Massimo for his losses to the wildfire. Massimo said that he, his wife and two teenaged kids were staying in the guesthouse of a relative who owned a ranch in Hollister.

Massimo looked to be in his 40s, with short, thick black hair, a square face which gravity had already started remodeling into jowls, oversized ears, and dark bags under weary brown eyes. He made me think of a basset hound.

"They told us to evacuate, so I sent the wife and kids off in the afternoon and sent the staff home. I figured it was just a precaution, you know, we were probably going to be fine. Never had a fire up there in all the years our family's owned the land. And the fire was a few ridges off and heading away from us. But the shit hit the fan around 4 a.m. when the wind shifted. There must have been some nearby hotspots and before I knew it, it was coming up over our ridge. Good thing I was doing sentry duty. I got out just in time.

"Anyway, as you can probably imagine, I'm up to my eyeballs in crap I gotta deal with. So let's get right to it, okay?"

Fine with me. "How can I help you?"

"You got any kids, Brink?"

"No, I don't."

"Well, if you ever do, do them a favor. Don't leave them any joint property in your will."

I wrote JOINT PROPERTY on my client intake form and said, "I'll be sure to remember that."

"Right. So here goes. My kid brother Gianni is my only sibling. Our parents got COVID right in the beginning. They both died from it. We inherited 50-50."

He must have noticed me jotting down notes, because he said, "That's spelled G-I-A-N-N-I."

I wrote, GIANNI PRONOUNCED JOHNNY. "Isn't that how it usually works?"

"Huh?"

I looked down at my notes. "Inheritance. Two siblings. 50-50."

"Yeah. Sure. It was a simple will my parents had. But joint property..." He pulled a face and shook his head. "Don't do it. Remember that for the sake of your kids. I'm executor of the estate. Most of it was tied up in Piscatelli Vineyards. They shoulda set it up so I bought Gianni out over time. Anyway, the vineyard's been in my family for generations. It's the only home I've ever known, the only place I've ever worked. I went to Davis, got a degree in viticulture and enology, then came back home. Been running the business with my old man ever since. I mean, until he passed."

I wrote, DAVIS-VITICULTURE & WINEOLOGY. It was what I had heard.

"Anyways, for me, taking over when Mom and Dad died was the natural thing. Gianni was another story. I'm the older brother, the responsible, reliable one. But Gianni's always done his own thing. He writes mystery novels, always travelling to scout out locations and characters for his stories. Never showed any interest in the family business."

He shook his head. "We talked it over. He said he was happy to be a silent partner. Which was fine by me. We agreed to split the profits, on top of which I got a nice salary. Only now there is no business, just acres of ashes. Piscatelli Vineyards is as good as bankrupt."

I nodded. Massimo was the one who wanted to get right down to business. Not that this wasn't useful information, but I wondered when he would get to the point.

"Now I'm battling the insurance company, but even though I can act without Gianni's agreement for most things, these insurance weenies say they need to deal with both partners."

Massimo stopped, as if it was now obvious why he needed my services. I'm a trained detective; I detected that it was time to use my powers of deduction. "Dealing with Gianni is a problem?"

"You might say. I haven't heard from him since shortly after the funeral. That's not unusual, he'd always disappear for a while, like I said, doing research for his next book. We might not hear from him for weeks or months. Then he'd come back and hole up in his cottage, writing.

"Now he's been away half a year. Longest time ever. And it's become urgent. I don't know where he is. He doesn't respond to texts or email. My calls just go to voicemail, which is not unusual, he mostly keeps his phone off so he can't be tracked because he's paranoid about shit like that. But he usually answers my messages eventually, only he hasn't. Longest time ever he's gone radio silent.

"So, yeah, you could say that dealing with Gianni's a big fucking problem. That's why I need you, Brink. I need you to find Gianni. Fast."

I wrote, FIND GIANNI!

Life Is Never Easy

* * *

Thankfully, Massimo's insurer was not one I did work for, so I had no conflict of interest. I asked if he had talked to a lawyer about dealing with them, particularly with a missing partner.

He shook his head and wagged a finger at me. "No lawyers. Never use them. Like my daddy always said, they only complicate and slow things down while they run up their bill."

I refrained from saying that a good lawyer might have given his parents better advice and prepared better estate planning documents, thus avoiding Massimo's current dilemma. Who was I to argue with my client when I was about to become the beneficiary of that inherited familial lawyer avoidance syndrome?

Especially when he had his checkbook out. Metaphorically.

* * *

In a new first in my PI career, I had to sign an NDA before Massimo would tell me anything else about what Gianni did for a living. However, lest you think this legalistic requirement odd for a staunch anti-lawyer adherent, it was a generic, fill-in-the-blanks NDA form that was free on the Internet. No lawyer involved.

While Massimo took a break, I printed the form,

signed, scanned and emailed it to him. A moment later, he was back. Much to my surprise, he revealed that his brother, Gianni Bernardo Piscatelli, wrote the popular Jack Bernard mystery series under the penname Sir Dean Fisher. Massimo emphasized that Sir Dean Fisher's real identity was a closely held secret.

"Gianni loves word games," Masimo said. "Piscatelli means little fish. Family legend is that our Italian ancestors fished for sardines. So, Sir Dean Fisher. Cute, huh?" The way he said it, with a sour face like he had been sucking a lemon, I gathered that Massimo did not appreciate cute.

I had read one of the Jack Bernard mystery novels, but I didn't care for it. Set in the 1960s, the plot centers around a serial killer who left clues, riddles, to taunt the police. PI Bernard and his partner spend much of their time deciphering these clues which turn out to be anagrams. The partner's name is Bella. Which is short for Annabelle. Last name, Graham. A.k.a. Anna Graham. I could understand Massimo's disdain, the whole thing was way too cutesy for my taste.

Massimo drew a blank when I asked about Gianni's friends, lovers, or other relatives he might be close to. "Gianni's extremely shy, a real loner," he said, "He doesn't do relationships. You gotta communicate with people when they're not with you to do that. Not his thing."

Life Is Never Easy

He said that when he wasn't off doing fieldwork research, Gianni lived in a cottage on the Piscatelli Vineyards property. Or had. Massimo assured me that the cottage, along with any records or other clues he might have kept there, had been destroyed. Nothing but a pile of ashes for a PI to search. Which I still planned to do as soon as the fire was controlled well enough so they would let me.

"Besides, Gianni does everything paperless, in the cloud. And he never gets anything but junk mail at the house, uses a PO box because he travels so much and, like I said, he's kinda paranoid about anyone knowing his business." Massimo said he had no idea about any of Gianni's passwords for online services, or his credit card or checking account information. Nor had Gianni ever disclosed details of his past travels, let alone his plans before he went AWOL.

All in all, not much to go on. However, Gianni may not have done relationships, but he had a literary agent who had a web page. Which had her contact information.

It was a place to start.

Chapter 4

I picked up a double cheeseburger, fries, and a shake from Greasy Jack's. The air was thick with smoke and ash from the wildfire still raging not far away. I hoped the mask I wore outside to ward off the virus was also protecting me from inhaling that junk.

While I ate lunch at my desk, I checked out Gianni's online presence. That did not take long. He had none.

I had never realized that Sir Dean Fisher was a penname. Or that he wasn't British. And not a Peer of the Realm. I could not find anything useful online about Gianni under his penname, not even a single photo, just the brief bio blurb that appeared on Sir Dean's author website and in his books which revealed next to nothing: *Sir Dean Fisher is author of the Jack Bernard mystery series. He now resides in California, where he does most of his writing on a remote mountaintop.* Maybe they were charged by the word. Also no photos or social media.

As I was finishing lunch, Cora Mott, Gianni's literary agent, returned my call. I told her who I was and that I was trying to find her missing client because of a family emergency. She made a funny sound when I said I worked for Massimo but quickly covered it and asked me to email her a copy of the NDA I had signed; Gianni's inner circle seemed serious about protecting his identity. A few minutes later, she called me back.

"So, you're looking for the elusive Sir Dean? Join the club," she said. "His editor and his publisher have been hounding me. I mean, he's not the only reclusive writer, far from it, or the only oddball one, but this is extreme even for him."

Mott went on to confirm what Massimo had told me, that Gianni's pattern was to disappear and go incommunicado for weeks or months at a time while he travelled doing research. Then he would surface, call Mott, tell her about the next book, and head home to write it while she worked on a short summary.

"When did you last hear from him?"

"Sometime in March. He'd just lost his parents and said he needed to get back to work, he needed the distraction."

"Had he been working on a new book?"

"So he said. His contract is for a book a year. A draft of this year's is overdue. He told me he had a real good idea he was working on before he went silent. But not what it was. He's like that."

"You have any idea where he might have gone?"

"Not a clue. But there is one thing."

"What's that?"

"When you find him, tell him to contact me right away or I'll kick his skinny little butt."

* * *

I called Boomer and told him why Massimo had hired me.

"Makes sense," Boomer said. "Explains why he was asking me and Sarge if we had any idea where the kid was. Which we don't."

Gianni was older than me, but I guess at Boomer's age, a lot of us are kids. "What can you tell me about Gianni?"

"Quiet fella," Boomer said. "He'd come over and just sort of hang out, maybe ask some questions about explosives, you know, stuff he might use in a book. Lent me a hand a few times with some of my experiments."

"Did he come by often?"

"Nah. Wouldn't see him for ages, then he'd show up out of the blue."

"When did you see him last?"

"Not long after his parents' funeral. That was here on the boat when he bought Sarge's RV."

"He bought Sarge's RV?"

"What I said. Sarge hadn't driven it since we got back from that Manning Cross adventure and face it, he knew he wasn't ever going to drive it again. He's too old. Slow. Distracted. Gets confused. Unlike yours truly."

"Did he say what he planned to use it for, maybe a trip he was planning?"

"Just that he liked to travel around the country and wanted to give the RV thing a try."

I got Sarge on the call. He confirmed what Boomer had told me. He too had no idea where Gianni might have been heading.

The guys didn't seem to have anything more to offer that might help my investigation, so I changed tack. "Last time we talked, I got the impression you might have a health issue, Boomer."

"Ah, yeah, well, I seem to have what they call long COVID."

"I thought you'd had a mild case and recovered."

"True, but I still can't smell worth a damn, and I get these headaches."

"You've seen a doctor?"

"Yeah, Pappa Joe. Doc says they're seeing this a lot. Folks get well but annoying symptoms just linger. But they don't have enough experience with the virus to know more, like how long this might last."

"I'm sorry to hear that," I said.

"Not half as sorry as me. Food tastes like cardboard when you can't smell. Anyway, when are you going to check my place?"

I had promised Boomer I'd check out his property.

Not for an insurance claim; since he wasn't living there anymore, Boomer had let his policy lapse. He figured most of the value was in the land anyway, and what could happen to that? "As soon as they give us access. The roads up the mountain are still blocked. It's not safe yet. It's a day-to-day thing."

"From what Piscatelli told me, you probably won't find much left," he said. "Never had a fire up there before that I can remember. Never thought we would. Good thing we don't have to live there anymore."

"Seems like a hard place to fight a fire," I said.

"Hard to get away in a hurry, too."

"Would you have evacuated?"

"I want to say yes; I'm no dummy."

"But?"

"Probably would've waited 'til the last minute, like Piscatelli."

Chapter 5

I had a Zoom appointment that evening with Dr. Shelly. I liked that I could see his whole face. My psychotherapist rarely said much, so reading his expressions was important to me. That would have been hard to do if we had met in person with masks on. Which we still couldn't do anyway.

Not long after the *Sweetwater* Showdown, I had a session with Dr. Shelly. It was the first time I had killed someone—hopefully, the last—and I was feeling surprisingly okay about it, though perhaps I should not have been surprised, given the kill-or-be-killed circumstances. At the time, I couldn't decide if my equanimity was a good or bad thing and sought out my therapist to help me sort it out.

Two things had come out of that session. First, my rational mind was convinced I had complete justification for my actions that day. Had I not shot Sean Corrigan when I did, the thug would have killed me without hesitation, and Boomer and Sarge would have followed shortly thereafter.

Second, I had no disturbing feelings about having taken Corrigan's life. Intellectually, I thought I should be devastated, but I wasn't. I was a little sad, sure, but if other negative feelings were there, I had successfully walled them off.

Dr. Shelly and I had agreed that I would not dwell on the matter but would be vigilant for symptoms that might indicate that I needed to deal with the issue again. After the depression I had fallen into after Anna, the love of my life, died, I had a sense of what those symptoms might be like. So when I had trouble sleeping for several days—it was why I had been awake at 4 a.m. to hear the thunder and, according to Boomer, the sound of his barn blowing up—I scheduled the appointment.

* * *

As usual, the ball was in my court. "I slept fine last night," I said.

Dr. Shelly waited. Whenever he did that, which was often, he kept very still, appeared to be totally present with me and content to wait for as long as it took for me to say something useful.

"So," I continued, "what was different about last night?" *See, I've learned this shrink stuff.* "Nothing really. Today was an interesting day, but yesterday was sort of ho-hum."

Life Is Never Easy

Dr. Shelly did something with his forehead and eyebrows. I took it to mean, *You're stalling, Joe.*

"Okay, so about my insomnia. It started a week or so ago. It isn't nightmares disturbing my sleep, not like the ones I used to have about Anna. I just lie there for hours before I finally fall asleep, then I'm wiped out the next day."

This time, I got a raised eyebrow.

"It's possible that I'm having bad dreams but don't remember them," I said.

Dr. Shelly was onto my avoidance. I was, however unintentionally, circling around the important thing. He took pity on me. "What's going on when you lie in bed not falling asleep?"

"I keep thinking about all the crazy things going on. The pandemic. The economic collapse. The drought. The heat. The fires. Bad air quality. Climate change in general. Black people being shot by police. Urban rioting. Trump and the election. Round and round like that."

"So, not Joe Brink killing a man," Dr. Shelly said. It was not a question.

"No. Not that."

"Anything in that litany you can do much about."

"Nope."

"Do you usually ruminate like that?"

"Just the opposite. I focus on things I *can* do something about and figuring out what to do about them."

"Even when it keeps you from falling asleep?"

"Sure, that happens. But then I usually either work out a plan or decide to sleep on it. I don't normally have much trouble falling asleep when I want to. Which is why I'm here."

"But last night?"

"I was looking forward to working out of my office for the first time since the shutdown. It was more symbolic than anything, but I felt like I was finally getting back some control of my business."

A raised eyebrow. *Listen to what you just said, Joe.*

"Oh, I see," I said. "Control."

"Anxiety over loss of control. You could not control the actions of that man you shot in self-defense," Dr. Shelly said.

We sat in silence for a bit. "You know I hate guns. I don't own one, never carry one." It had been an issue in my relationship with Anna. She knew how dangerous my work could be and wanted me to be able to protect myself.

Dr. Shelly waited.

"And I killed a man with a gun."

He waited.

"Do you know how many gun metaphors we use all the time?"

"Go ahead," Dr. Shelly said, "shoot." He smiled at his little joke.

"Yeah," I said, "like that. Dodged a bullet. Fire the

gun. Jump the gun. Caught in a crossfire. Aim high. Hotshot. I could go on and on."

He waited.

"We have more guns than people in this country. By far the most per capita in the world. Like, ten times more than most countries. It's the Second Amendment gone wild. It's crazy."

He waited.

"And I can't control any of that," I said.

Chapter 6

Next morning, though the fire was still far from contained, the wind had shifted, the smoke and ash had cleared, the sky was bright blue, and I could once again breathe outside without getting a sinus headache. For the first time since the fires started, I was able to take my morning run.

Afterwards, I took a shower in Sally Rocket's still locked-down studio, which was across the hall from my office, on the second floor of an aging building the chamber of commerce called quaint, over a fro-yo shop and a bakery. I had a key and her bathroom, unlike the one in my office, had a shower. Sally taught self-defense, mainly to women, but her methods were very much in-person and hands-on, and she had to close when the pandemic hit.

Feeling energized and eager to face the day for the first time in many weeks, I went downstairs and got a bagel with cream cheese from the bakery and a Rocket Smoothie—named after Sally—from the fro-yo shop. Both stores had managed to survive the lockdown on

Life Is Never Easy

takeout business and some government aid. Back upstairs, I ate second breakfast at my desk.

The authorities were not going to let us into the fire zone until it was under better control. So we had at least several days before Ricky could start taking pictures of the damage and I could check out Boomer's and Piscatelli's properties.

So, time to dig into Gianni Piscatelli. I knew the cops would be uninterested in even taking a missing person's report for an adult with a history of going off incommunicado, particularly one who had purchased an RV just before disappearing. They sure wouldn't do more than file it even if they did.

I used an online service to comb through the various domestic death certificate databases. There was no record of a Piscatelli dying anywhere in the United States since March when Gianni vanished. I then tried Dean Fisher and Jack Bernard, because why not? The search engine automatically checked for similar spellings of names, and I got a few hits, but none close in age to Gianni's.

The RV revelation reminded me that I had forgotten to ask Massimo what kind of car his brother drove and any details he might know about it. When I called and asked him about it, he said, "Didn't I tell you he had bought the RV from Sarge and taken off in it? I mean, he said he would, so he must have. What's left of his burned-out old Honda is still parked next to the cottage."

I was certain he had never mentioned any of that but decided against confronting him about it. Instead, I reminded Massimo that he owed me a recent photo of Gianni and a list of people who knew him. Relatives, friends, vineyard staff, doctor, dentist, schoolteachers, college roommates. Whoever he could think of, regardless of whether the relationship was close. He reminded me how reclusive and unsocial his brother was; I reminded him that I could never predict where a clue would come from.

"You'll have it all in the morning," he grumbled, and ended the call.

I called Sarge. "Do you remember how Gianni paid for the RV?"

"I don't take credit cards and I'd sure remember if he paid cash. Must have been a check."

With a lot of patient help from me, Sarge logged into his bank account, retrieved an image of the check he had deposited, and emailed it to me. I now knew where Gianni banked and his account number. And had a sample of his signature. This was information I had been unable to get from Massimo, who had insisted he had never written Gianni a check and vice-versa. Which seemed odd but...

In any case, along with the bank information from Sarge, Massimo and Cora Mott had given me the same

Life Is Never Easy

mobile number and email address for Gianni. Sarge had also given me the model, color, and other information about the RV. I had some solid leads. I got ready to spend some quality time digging around online, sometimes in places I was not supposed to enter. If I got stuck, I could always enlist Jonathan and Charles, my neighbors who were white-hat hackers, meaning, as they said, that they used their powers to do good. Or to help a friend.

But first, I was going to run a background check on Massimo Piscatelli. I had learned the hard way that clients routinely lie or withhold information for all manner of reasons, and more than one had turned out to be criminally involved in the very case they hired me to investigate. This included committing murder. One had even tried to shoot me in my office to silence me.

The *PI Handbook* quotes the Russian proverb: *Doveryay, no proveryay.* "Trust, but investigate."

* * *

Sally called. The lockdown was getting to her.

"I can't work, can't go anywhere, and I'm climbing the walls here," she said.

"I'm back in the office," I said. I told her about the fire insurance work and the Piscatelli case.

"How about I help Ricky," she said. "You still got your backup camera?"

"I do. That's a great idea. But it'll be a few days."

"Give me something to look forward to, you know, anticipate the excitement. And making a few bucks wouldn't hurt."

"Well, try to control yourself. Say, have you heard anything from your cousin?" We always referred to her sister Angie as Sally's unnamed cousin in case the FBI was listening. Not that I thought they would be, but you could never be sure. And it made Sally feel better.

"Nope," Sally said. "You know how she is."

I did. Angie was paranoid. For good reason. She was a fugitive, wanted by the Federal Bureau of Investigation of the United States of America. For at least one murder. Which she had admittedly committed.

Chapter 7

Zooming with Joan Piscatelli.

"My brother-in-law is a spoiled, self-absorbed little shit. His saving grace is he's usually gone, and when he's here, he's mostly invisible."

Ah, familial love! Merely introducing myself had been enough to prompt this outpouring. I was unsure whether to encourage her to continue ranting or try to tamp down the emotional energy. Sometimes people reveal more when passion overcomes their normal filters. On the other hand, venting can interfere with their ability to think clearly and provide useful information. It was a tossup. I employed my favorite move when undecided what to say. I kept my mouth shut.

Unaware of my quandary, Joan rolled on. "Who spoiled him? I'll tell you who. His mother. Gianni was Eva's baby, she catered to his every need. Meanwhile, Massimo was the dutiful first child, always worked in the vineyard as a kid, got the education he needed to take over, worked his ass off making sure everyone else was taken care of. Then they leave the business to both of them? How unfair is that? Gianni doesn't lift a finger to help out, just keeps mooching off us while he plays mystery writer. And what thanks does Massimo get? I'll tell you what thanks. None."

I thought she had wound down, but she was just pausing for breath.

"Then he goes off in a huff, leaves my husband to run the show by himself, not that the waste of space would be any help, he's useless. But what about showing just a little responsibility? And why? Because Massimo put him in his place at the funeral? He needed to be told what's what. It was about time."

I waited a beat to see if she had more, but the air had finally run out of the balloon, and it lay flat on the floor.

I asked my questions, but Joan had little to add to what Massimo had already told me that might be of help locating Gianni. Before ending the interview, I said, "Can you tell me more about the argument at the funeral?"

"Not much to tell. It was after. People were leaving the gravesite, but the brothers had walked off together. I figured they needed some space alone, you know, losing their parents like that and all. But it was obvious they were arguing. They were too far away to hear what they were saying, but you could hear raised voices. It was embarrassing. The whole thing took just a few minutes. They came back, we all got in the car like nothing had happened. Except they weren't talking to each other."

"Did Massimo tell you what was said?"

"He just said that things would have to change. But that Gianni was a stubborn fool."

"What did you take that to mean?"

"Why is this important?"

"I never know what might be important," I said.

"Okay. What I thought was that he told his brother he would have to pull his weight in the business, but Gianni refused."

"What did you think when he took off?"

"I thought it was typical Gianni, just thinking about himself. And now when he's really needed, he's nowhere to be found."

* * *

I called Massimo that evening to update him on my progress. It was good that he was impatient and uninterested in details, because I had little of substance to tell him.

But I did have a question. "I hear that you and Gianni had a bit of an altercation at your parents' funeral. Can you tell me what it was about?"

"What's that got to do with finding him?"

"Didn't he go missing shortly afterwards?"

"Well, yeah, but…"

I repeated my mantra, reminding him yet again that

I could never tell where a clue would come from.

"Well, I'll tell you what it was about. It was about what killed our folks: COVID. And about him refusing to wear a mask even after that happened..."

Massimo paused. I waited.

"I may have told him to keep away from us unless he'd mask-up."

"Keep away as in self-isolating? Or keep away from home entirely?"

"Hmm. You know, I may have sort of implied he should stay away from my family until he could behave responsibly. Which he didn't do. Mask up, I mean. But I let it slide, and soon he was gone..."

It wasn't exactly a clue, but it was sure interesting. I was pretty sure Massimo was bullshitting me, but one thing for sure: he and his wife had not coordinated their stories.

Chapter 8

On Friday, September 9, 2020. I woke up on another planet.

It was a dark world with a hazy orange sky but no sun. I went out for my morning run and found the air surprisingly free of smoke, but I cut my run short because it felt so weird outside. On the news, they said it was caused by the high smoke from the many wildfires throughout the region reflecting some of the light from the sun that makes the sky look blue, letting through the orange wavelengths. Whatever, it was just plain creepy.

Oddly, this signaled the end of the restrictions on access to the area that Brink Investigations had been assigned to survey for the insurance company; the fire was well-enough contained. And so it was that my little team headed into the Santa Cruz Mountains. We were in separate cars. Sally and Ricky had quite a few days of work ahead of them photographing property damage from the fire. But I didn't plan to stay long. I had promised Boomer I would personally check his place, after which I planned to get back to work on the Gianni Piscatelli case.

Off the freeway south of Los Gatos, I took Bear Creek Road, which I followed west in the direction of Boulder Creek until it narrowed into a series of harrowing curves bordered by sheer drops on one side and the dense redwood forest on the other. No matter how often I had been there, I still had to carefully pick my way onto a series of nearly hidden, unnamed, narrow, twisting roads that connected at unexpected places. Always climbing. Slowly. Though I could not let my concentration on the road ahead waiver for a second, I was keenly aware of the destruction around me. Unlike in the lowlands, where the smoke had dissipated, up there I could not only smell it, I could taste it.

When I finally reached Boomer's property, I was stunned. All that remained of his cabin was a stone chimney surrounded by ash-covered rubble. The barn that had stood behind the cabin had been reduced to a mound of charred debris. The once lush and towering redwoods that had dotted the residence area, as well as those in the surrounding dense forest, pointed stubby blackened fingers at the heavens as if in accusation.

Wearing protective gear, taking photos with my phone for Boomer, I walked around the remains of the cabin, then headed to what had been the barn. The roof had collapsed onto whatever had been inside. Which included the blackened husk of an RV. Next to which I

Life Is Never Easy

discovered the incinerated remains of what was once a human being.

I had found Gianni.

* * *

The detective who caught the case had spoken with me at the scene. The next day, I was giving my formal statement.

I could tell that Detective Azevedo was pleased at the tidy package I had handed him, because he said, "That's a nice, tidy package, Brink."

Azevedo referred to his notebook and read like he was going through a checklist. "Six months ago, the property owner, Edgar Montana, and his roommate, Stan Zampisi, move onto a boat in San Francisco. Gianni Piscatelli, who lives next door to the Montana property, buys the RV that Zampisi garaged in the barn. As is his habit, Gianni takes off for parts unknown. Then comes the fire. Gianni's brother, Massimo Piscatelli, who also lives next door, asks Montana to put him in touch with this PI Montana knows, which happens to be you, because he needs Gianni's help dealing with the aftermath of the fire. You come here to check on the property for your friend Montana. Discover the corpse. Call 9-1-1. And here we are."

Where we were was a police interview room, but I chose not to point that out. I knew what Detective

Azevedo meant and had no desire to annoy him.

I had given him the bare facts as I understood them. No mention of the reported funeral incident. And nothing about an explosion. They were not facts, just hearsay.

* * *

They recovered the VIN from the vehicle. It was Gianni's, the one he had bought from Sarge. It appeared that Gianni had been parked in the barn, though no one could say for how long. No one else I could find had been on the property for months. Other than those going to and from Piscatelli Vineyards next door, the last property on the remote road, no one had any reason to even pass by. And no one associated with Piscatelli Vineyards could recall spotting the RV or seeing anyone, let alone Gianni, coming or going from Boomer's place.

Regardless, he was in there that night when the fire came around 4 a.m. Whether he had been asleep inside the RV or not, he died before he could get out of the barn. A tragic accident.

Massimo called and thanked me for my efforts. He said he had formally identified the body. Although it was burned beyond recognition, the medallion Gianni always wore around his neck was still intact.

"Are you sure it was Gianni's?"

Life Is Never Easy

"Yeah, he had it custom made a long time ago. Just the word LINE in capital letters engraved on a silver disc. He called it his dog tag. Wore it all the time."

"Why line?"

"It was another of Gianni's word games from when he was a kid. He told everyone it stood for 'Life is never easy' but it was way more complicated than that."

"How so?"

"Got a pad and pen?"

I did.

"Write it down. All caps. Nothing between the letters. LINE."

I did.

"So, what did you just do?"

"I wrote the word line."

"And you capitalized it, right?"

"You told me to."

This was getting silly.

"Okay, Brink. Now write these two words: capitalizing line."

"Okay, I did."

"You remember Gianni's penname? Sir Dean Fisher? Supposed to be a Brit, right? They spell capitalize with an s, not a z. And that's my last clue. You're a detective, Brink, you figure it out."

With that, he ended the call.

Then I stared at my pad for a long time. Nothing happened. So I turned to my anagram app. Bingo!

Phil Bookman

CAPITALISINGLINE
GIANNIPISCATELLI

I sent Massimo my invoice.

Chapter 9

Boomer was devastated. He believed the explosion had killed Gianni. But I convinced him that we should keep that speculation to ourselves. I emphasized that word: speculation. There was no point sharing Massimo's unverified story with the police. Just the facts.

Which turned out to be a futile effort, because, unbeknownst to us, Massimo had let the cat out of the bag when he first spoke with Detective Azevedo. Azevedo, as cops are inclined to do, had not shared that tidbit with me. But he did share it with the DA's office.

The citizens of California were growing increasingly alarmed by wildfires and had little patience with those whose actions might contribute to them. Nor was there a constituency for elderly explosives experts. And the district attorney was an ambitious political animal.

A month after I found Gianni Piscatelli's corpse, they charged Boomer with negligent homicide. A felony. Punishable by a fine and up to four years in prison.

* * *

I was attorney Ed Wax's primary investigator, his go-to guy, although he had not had any work for me for months. With the courts mostly closed, the pandemic had slashed the demand for the kind of legal work that required an investigator. I knew he was representing Boomer and I was anxious to help my friend.

I called Ed. As always, he got right to the point.

"You can't work on Boomer's case. Clear conflict of interest."

He went on in his usual machine-gun delivery over the phone, firing bullet points. "Your former client appears to be the only witness to the alleged explosion. You investigated the deceased. Clear conflicts."

And that was that. Or so Ed thought.

* * *

The Internet, as they say, lost its mind.

An aging vet named Boomer with a secret explosives laboratory hidden in the backwoods on a remote mountain top. Living in luxury on a superyacht in San Francisco harbor. With another Viet Nam vet of questionable background named Sarge. The pair who, along with PI Joe Brink, were involved in the infamous *Sweetwater* Showdown last spring. During which Brink shot and killed drug kingpin Rick Varga. And the

Life Is Never Easy

yacht belongs to Silicon Valley moneyman Nick Marchetti's company. The same Nick Marchetti whose late uncle Vito Cangelosi had ruled the New York City docks for the mafia for decades. The same Nick Marchetti who was once wanted by the FBI in connection with the murder of tech billionaire Barry Samson.

It was all juicy red meat for conspiracy theorists and rabble rousers of all stripes, and they flooded the Internet with ever-more inflammatory posts. That Boomer and Sarge were murderers was, it seemed, a given. More, they were connected to all manner of nefarious organizations and infamous events. That Boomer had been so lightly charged and Sarge not at all, was taken as a sure sign of a government coverup, probably a conspiracy. And so it went ad nauseum.

The good news was that the president was not pleased by being upstaged by these two California geezers, especially with the election close at hand, and quickly reasserted his God-given right to command all attention, all the time. After a few days, the Internet refocused on the big cheese's big show, along with whatever the Kardashians were up to, and interest in Boomer and the rest of it petered out. Temporarily.

* * *

There was another piece of good news. The brouhaha pissed off Nick Marchetti, who called me to tell me so.

"This sucks, Joe. They dig up all that old shit about my family and the Barry Samson nonsense and spread it all over. And there's no way to stop them."

Nick ranted a bit more, then thanked me for letting him get it off his chest. He also reminded me not to respond online to any of it. That only would serve to feed the beast. I assured him I knew that.

As I suspected, Nick was bankrolling Boomer's legal defense. "Ed won't let me work on the case for him," I said. "Conflict of interest."

"I know," Nick said, "Ed told me. But I you won't leave it at that, right?"

"He's my friend." That said it all.

"Just watch your ass. And look, I'm willing to do whatever it takes to clear Boomer, so if you get any ideas I can help with, let me know."

Chapter 10

The sky had almost returned to normal, and the air was getting less smokey every day. But still hazy, like Boomer's future.

"Boomer cannot go to prison," Sally said. "We have to help him." Sally and I were in my office, seated across from each other at my desk. Sally, who had been abandoned at a young age by both her parents and grown up in foster homes of various shades of oppressive, had a special relationship with Boomer. He was the grandfather she never had.

Ed had gotten Boomer released right away on bail. No one in authority seemed to want a man pushing 80 with long COVID in jail, at least not before he had been convicted. Boomer had to surrender his passport, wear an ankle monitor, and stay at home, in his case meaning onboard *Sweetwater*.

I may have been officially off the case, but I was not about to add Boomer's fate to the long list of things that haunted me but that I was helpless to control.

I also had an insight without another session with

Dr. Shelly. The issue for me was not about being in complete control of a situation, it was being able to do something to resolve or at least improve it, whatever it was. I knew that I could not assure my friend was cleared. But since I was officially off the case, I could and would do things that Ed and his team could not. Of course, as a licensed PI, I faced ethical restrictions, but they were trumped by Joe Brink's Golden Rule: *Do for your friend that which your friend would do for you.*

I told Sally that. "I'm all in," I said. "But Boomer won't talk to me. He said he doesn't want to put me in jeopardy."

"He'll talk to me," Sally said. "Already has. He said Ed only told him not to talk to you."

"That'll work," I said. "I'm sure Ed will have a good investigator on the case, so I think we shouldn't duplicate that work."

Sally looked confused. "I thought you said…"

"So," I forged on, "we do what Ed and his investigator can't or won't do."

"I don't understand," Sally said.

Then I told her about my conversation with Nick, and the one I'd had that morning with Uncle Bill.

* * *

Uncle Bill was actually my father's uncle, my great-uncle. He and Aunt Flo lived in a retirement community near Palm Springs, where they had moved after Bill retired after a long career as an Assistant District Attorney in L.A. When I had a question about criminal law, Uncle Bill was my go-to guy. He was also the only one in the family, aside from my mom, who called me Joey.

We were on a video call. Uncle Bill looked a bit grayer each time I saw him, but that appeared to be his only concession to aging.

"It's good to see you, Joey. How's the lockdown been for you?"

We exchanged some small talk. He told me that Aunt Flo was out doing something with some friends, he wasn't sure exactly who or what; he couldn't keep track of the groups and clubs she belonged to. Then I told him about Boomer's situation and my conflict-of-interest.

"Yeah, I heard something about that. You're in the news again."

"Do you have time to help me figure out what I *can* do to help my friend?"

"Joey, the thing about being retired is I have nothing but time. Let me go get a beer and then we can talk." He soon returned with a can in his hand. "I sure hope your friend's lawyer gets the judge to rule that they cannot refer to your friend as Boomer during the trial. Too prejudicial. Assuming that's a nickname, although you can't be sure these days."

"His name's Edgar Montana," I said.

"Okay then. So here's how the trial would go. First, the prosecution will offer evidence that there was an explosion, including testimony from that guy you said saw it and a CSI. Maybe also an explosives expert. The defense will have its own expert to try to refute that, and maybe impeach the eyewitness. They're notoriously unreliable."

"No explosion, no crime," I said.

"Right. Then the prosecution will offer evidence that Boomer had illegally stored dangerous material. From what you've told me, that could be hard to refute."

"Lots of people knew about it," I said.

"Next, a prosecution expert will testify that those chemicals caused the explosion. The defense expert will contradict that. It would be helpful if the RV had a propane tank that exploded, or maybe the gas tank."

"If there was an explosion but Boomer's chemicals didn't cause it, no crime," I said.

"Right. Now for the biggie. Did the explosion cause the victim's death? If the medical examiner says it did, the defense will have an expert to say the ME is wrong, or at least could be wrong. But I bet the ME would waffle about cause of death, particularly if the body was as badly burned as you tell me. So that's another point for a defense expert to raise, like maybe he had a heart attack trying to escape the fire and died before he could get out of the barn, maybe even before the alleged explosion. All sorts of possibilities for defense mischief there."

"If there was an explosion and Boomer's chemicals caused it, but it didn't kill Gianni, no crime," I said.

"You have a way with words, Joey. Maybe you should have been a lawyer. Anyway, the defense in this case would be all about reasonable doubt. It could all come down to a battle of the experts. It's always a crapshoot taking a case like that to a jury. You can never tell what'll happen. So it's wise not to let it get to trial. The best thing would be to take a plea and pay a fine with no jail time."

"I'm sure Ed Wax will try to do that," I said. "But I have the impression the DA wants to make an example of Boomer, what with all the fires."

"You could be right about that. The politics don't favor your friend."

"What about Gianni trespassing? He had no business being in the barn. So wasn't whatever happened to him his own fault?"

"You might think so, but you'd be wrong. The property owner is responsible if someone is injured, even a trespasser. Unless they are legally defending themselves."

"That seems wrong," I said.

"What can I say, it's the law. But look, if this Ed Wax is as good as you say, he'll handle everything we've talked about. Mainly, sow confusion. The more confusing the case, the better for the defense. What you should focus on is what he's not likely to do."

"What's that?"

Uncle Bill grinned. "Just give the prosecutor proof that someone else killed the victim before the explosion. And do it before the case goes to trial."

"Oh, is that all?"

"From what you told me you already have a suspect."

"I do?"

"The brother," Uncle Bill said. "The guy who says he saw the explosion. He seems to have a financial motive. Take a real close look at him for it."

"What if I do manage to prove he or someone else killed Gianni?"

"Find a way to get the evidence to the DA Maybe via Wax. Just do it so it can't be traced back to you to avoid your conflict-of-interest problem. Otherwise, you'll become the DA's focus and he'll go all out to discredit you and your evidence."

"Okay."

"And if all else fails, sow as much confusion as you can."

* * *

"So we assume Gianni was already dead when the fire came," Sally said, after I finished reviewing Uncle Bill's analysis for her. It wasn't a question.

"And we assume he didn't die of natural causes, an

accident, or suicide," I said. "If he did, Ed will cover that ground."

"Which means he was murdered," Sally said. "And we think that Massimo did it?"

I shrugged. "We start there. I got no other suspects, do you?"

"Nope," Sally said.

"And I keep a low profile," I said.

"The 'watch your ass' thing," Sally said. "You being a PI with a conflict and all. Whereas I'm just an ordinary civilian trying to help my friend out of a jam."

Sally and I spent the rest of the day reviewing the Piscatelli case file, but instead of thinking about "how does this help find Gianni?" we asked, "how does this help prove Massimo killed his brother?"

As we went along, we made a list of all the questions we wanted to answer, given our new point of view. After dinner—pizza delivered from MySlice—we divvied up our assignments.

When we were ready to pack it in, I said, "One more thing. We need a code name for this new case. How about we call it Plan B?"

"B for Boomer?"

"No," I said.

"The morning after pill?"

I laughed. "You ever watch the old TV series called *The Practice?*"

Sally shook her head. "Never heard of it."

"I binge watched it. It's about these defense lawyers. When they're losing a murder case at trial, they pick someone else to accuse and go after them full-bore right there in the courtroom. They don't care if the person is guilty or innocent, just that they can make them look guilty in the eyes of the jury and get their client off. They call it Plan B."

"Only we don't want to go to trial, and we want to nail the guilty party."

I noticed Sally had already made the mental switch to the assumption Gianni had been murdered. I wasn't quite there. Yet.

"Other than that," I said.

"Works for me," Sally said.

Chapter 11

When the case was about finding Gianni, the argument he and Massimo had at the funeral had seemed interesting but not terribly important. But it took on new meaning for Plan B.

Why didn't Massimo's wife know what they argued about? That is, assuming Massimo was telling the truth about the mask disagreement. Joan said she thought it was about Gianni's role in the business. Had she and Massimo not discussed the reason for the brothers causing a scene at their parents' funeral? Or had either Joan or Massimo intentionally misled me and simply failed to coordinate their stories?

Another thing. According to my notes, in our first interview Massimo said he and Gianni had talked after the funeral and that was when Gianni "happily agreed" to the silent partner role. No mention of any argument. Another inconsistency.

In any case, the way Joan described the scene, no one overheard what was actually said. Besides, the funeral had been immediate family only, and, being in stealth mode, I wanted to avoid dealing with them directly. So I decided to start with the bigger picture. How was the Piscatelli business doing before the fire?

It being a private, closely held family business, there was scant information available about Piscatelli Vineyards' financials. After a frustrating morning poking around online, I placed a call to Lisa Gold. She and her husband were one of Silicon Valley's legendary billionaire power couples. Mike Gold was the technology mogul; Lisa ran Duncan Gold Vineyards, their Napa-based wine business. I had gotten her number from Nick Marchetti, who was an old friend of the Golds as well as CFO of Mike's current venture. He had called Lisa to pave the way for me.

"Thank you for taking my call, Mrs. Gold," I began. "I don't know if you remember me, but Nick said it would be okay to call you directly."

"Please, Joe, it's Lisa, and of course I remember you. You're Nick's PI friend from Campbell. How can I help you?"

As it turned out, quite a bit.

* * *

I told Lisa Gold I was looking for financial information about Piscatelli Vineyards. I said that I could not tell her why and asked if she would keep my inquiry secret.

"What inquiry? I talk to so many people every day, I

can't possibly be expected to remember all the conversations I have."

"Thank you," I said.

"I also can't divulge certain things I might learn about in the course of my work. But I can tell you about a problem a family business *might* have. Hypothetically."

"I'd appreciate that."

"Okay. What sometimes happens is that a child grows up in the family business and learns the craft quite well. So as their parents age, they start taking over, especially the more physically demanding parts of the business. They focus on producing the product. Then the parents retire or pass away, and the child takes over completely."

That sure sounded familiar.

"Only they never really learned the other parts of the business or maybe they're just not good at certain things. But they're the only one from their generation available to run the show. The product's still good, but the business goes south because of their deficiencies. In fact, maybe it was already sliding downhill but the older generation was still around to shore things up.

"Now, let's suppose a buyer appears, one who only cares about acquiring the product. Maybe they're already in the business and want to expand capacity through acquisition. Maybe they've already approached the family before but were rebuffed. They offer the beleaguered owner a way out, probably sweeten the deal by offering to keep them on the payroll running the operation.

"There's just one small problem. There's another sibling who isn't involved in the business but inherited a share and flat-out won't agree to the sale."

I waited a beat, but Lisa Gold seemed to have arrived at the end of her story.

"That's very helpful," I said.

"And all hypothetical," she said.

* * *

There was one more detail I wanted to check on. I drove over to the county offices and asked to view Gianni Piscatelli's probate record. Sure enough, Massimo had filed it without the help of a lawyer. Gianni's will was a simple do it yourself form naming Massimo as executor and sole heir. So Massimo not only inherited Gianni's share of Piscatelli Vineyards, he also got whatever else was in Gianni's estate. Which, given Gianni's frugal lifestyle and successful career, could have been a tidy sum.

Some burden.

* * *

Life Is Never Easy

I got fish and chips delivered from Fishy Johnson for our dinner meeting at my condo. Sally had spent the day in San Francisco onboard *Sweetwater* with Boomer and Sarge. Like me, she had not seen them in person for months. "They're all alone except for us, Joe. I told the guys I was going to start visiting regularly. We've all had COVID already and I need to check on them in person."

"But you didn't say anything about Plan B."

Sally glared at me. "You think I'm a dummy?"

I put up my hands to ward her off. "Sorry. How are they doing?"

"Boomer's definitely got long COVID. He gets these chest pains, heart palpitations and shortness of breath. Says he never had them before. He takes his meds, and the doctor says there's nothing more to do for it but take it easy. Which he says he's getting good at."

"And Sarge?"

"His short-term memory is getting worse. He brings up the same thing we talked about an hour earlier like it's a new conversation. And he's getting aphasic, you know, losing his nouns, so he's even stingier with words. On the other hand, he tried to answer every question I asked him and never wanted to know why I was asking."

Sally paused, contemplating a particularly long French fry. "They're both real worried about the trial," Sally said, as if that revelation came from the super fry.

"And Boomer's torn up with guilt. It's different seeing them in person than on a Zoom call. I could tell it's eating at them both."

"If Plan B works, all that will go away," I said. "But it's a big if."

"About that, I found out Boomer refused to waive time. Against Ed's advice. Ed told Boomer that he could keep kicking the can down the road, maybe longer than Boomer has left to live. But Boomer doesn't want to be confined to that boat, lovely as it is, and doesn't want to live out his days with the trial hanging over him. They're looking to start the first week in December."

"So we're on deadline," I said. "Let's get at it. What did you find out?"

"I got the lowdown on the RV from Sarge. It seems Gianni was a germaphobe, and the pandemic made it a lot worse. He told Sarge he wanted to buy the RV so he could have a sanitary place to travel in and stay in. Which led to me to ask what he thought Gianni would think about masking, which was what I really wanted to know. The guys said he was all masked up when he came to complete the RV purchase. Even gave them a lecture about using better masks. And before you ask, they agreed this germ thing was not new behavior."

Which was more detail than Boomer and Sarge had given me before. Sometimes that was a problem with both of them. Verbally parsimonious.

"So Massimo lied to me," I said. "Which fits with

what I found out from Lisa Gold."

After I got off the call with Lisa Gold, I had spent some time online and discovered that she was on the board of a company called Grapewest Holdings. Grapewest touted themselves as the largest supplier of high-quality grapes to West Coast winemakers. Just the sort of outfit that might want to buy Piscatelli Vineyards. So she had not just been passing along a rumor. I told Sally that and filled her in on what Lisa Gold had told me.

"It sure changes things when you look at a case though a different lens," I said. "Massimo needs to sell the business before it goes under, but Gianni stands in the way. Gianni wants to keep the business and the land in the family, even though he doesn't want to be involved in it. They argue at the funeral. Maybe Massimo threatens Gianni. Anyway, Gianni buys the RV and takes off. So far, so good?"

"So far, so good," Sally said, nodding. "And how about this. The night of the fire, Gianni shows up. Massimo knows Gianni's coming; how doesn't matter. He has all the staff and his family evacuate, but he stays, waiting for Gianni. He's really pissed at Gianni because the fire is about to wipe out his home, his business, and his income. Oh, and maybe he also covets Gianni's nest egg. When Gianni arrives, Massimo kills him. Puts the body in the RV. Drives it to Boomer's barn. Positions the body. Spreads around some of Boomer's chemicals.

Maybe even sets the barn on fire as he leaves. Let's the advancing wildfire do the rest."

We were on a roll. "Massimo gets out as the fire closes in," I said. "He sees the explosion. Next day, he calls Boomer, then hires me to set up his story: the responsible big brother who needs to find his irresponsible little brother so he can salvage the family business."

Sally finished the last of her fish and chips and drained her beer. "It would work as a miniseries," she said.

I thought it sounded like a *Columbo* plot, but I kept that to myself. I doubted that Sally watched old *Columbo* shows like I did.

In any case, Sally was right. We had a great plot. We probably could sell it to some studio. What we didn't have was even a shred of hard evidence. Which we needed to sell it to the DA

I spent a sleepless night worrying how the hell we could get the proof we needed, all the while keeping Plan B under wraps. I finally got a couple of hours of sleep and woke up with a totally wild-ass idea.

Chapter 12

Mimosas and a Plastic Lei
A murder mystery about greed and sibling rivalry
By Sir Dean Fisher

This story is set in Hawaii in the 1960s when pineapple plantations were abundant. Two brothers have inherited the plantation that has been in their family for generations. Both live on the plantation. The older brother, married with children, who has a fondness for sipping mimosas and wearing a plastic lei, has been heavily involved in the business. The unmarried younger brother is an artist who paints tropical landscapes and makes a decent living but is not involved in the family business.

Due to the older brother's poor business skills, the plantation slides towards bankruptcy. Then the older brother receives an offer from a big company to buy the plantation, but his brother refuses to sell, insisting they owe it to their ancestors to keep it in the family.

Phil Bookman

The island's volcano erupts. As a lava flow threatens the plantation, the staff and family head to an evacuation center, leaving the brothers to take care of some last-minute items before they follow.

The older brother finally arrives at the evacuation center. But the younger brother, who he says had promised to come just as soon as he packed a few more things, never arrives. His lava-encased body is later recovered.

PI Jack Bernard and his partner Annabelle Graham are vacationing in Hawaii and are taken from their resort to the same evacuation center. They become involved and, in their inimitable style, untangle a series of baffling clues to uncover the fratricide and bring the older brother to justice.

* * *

"What do you think?"

Sally had brought burritos for lunch from Paco's Picante. "You wrote this?" she said, waving the page at me.

I gave Sally my aw-shucks shrug.

"All I can say is your vocabulary builder app has really worked wonders," Sally said. "This is good, Joe. And not subtle."

"I wasn't going for subtle. I tried to style it like the blurbs on Amazon for Gianni's books."

Life Is Never Easy

"What's the deal with mimosas and a lei?"

"A plastic lei," I said.

"I see. That makes all the difference in the world. What the hell does it mean?"

"You remember I told you Gianni was into word play and anagrams?"

"Yeah," Sally said. "And has a dopey-named sidekick in case anyone misses the point."

"Right. Anna Graham."

Sally picked up the paper and pondered.

"I don't get it."

"There's an app for anagrams, too," I said. "But good friend that I am, I will now reveal all. Mimosas is an anagram for Massimo."

Sally examined the page once more. I munched my burrito. "Wait. I see it now. Yeah, plastic lei is an anagram for Piscatelli."

"You learn well, grasshopper."

"Grasshopper?"

"*Kung Fu.* Another old TV series I binge watched during lockdown."

Eye roll. "You think Massimo will get the title?"

"I hope so," I said. "But he doesn't have to. He's bound to recognize the plot."

"You think this will work?"

"We'll find out soon," I said. "I think it's time to pull the trigger."

Hearing no objection, I sent Massimo an email containing the blurb. I used an anonymous service that would make tracing the sender and origin of the message impossible. Any reply would be rerouted to me. The subject of the email—*I know what you did*—was trite, but I did not care about originality, I only cared about effectiveness.

* * *

A lot of PI time is spent waiting. In this case, waiting for Massimo to reply to the email.

To pass the time, Sally and I discussed loose ends. Like, if our theory of the case was correct, how did Gianni drive the RV up the mountain the night of the explosion without being noticed by the police who had been directing evacuating traffic down Bear Creek Road and keeping people from going up?

Ricky Clancy, who had become an expert on those backroads, helped clear that up. Doing the insurance photo work, Ricky had discovered what he called the back way to get up the mountain, coming from the west on Big Basin Way through Saratoga instead of from the east off the freeway along Bear Creek Road. This route was the road less travelled. Ricky said the fire had never quite gotten there. So it was probably not getting the level of attention of the usual route that night.

Sally called Sarge and asked if he ever went that way.

Life Is Never Easy

He reminded her he hadn't driven in a long time, but that he had almost always gone that way because it had fewer hairpin turns and tight, narrow sections.

Our updated Plan B assumption was that Gianni had gone up the mountain the back way.

Another loose end: how had Gianni come to be there that night in the first place? Had Massimo lured him? Had he been in contact with Gianni all along? Or had Gianni somehow heard about the emergency and rushed home? We couldn't know.

We decided to assume Gianni wanted to get his stuff before the fire came and had alerted Massimo that he was coming. But it really didn't matter, any more than how exactly Massimo had killed him. Just that he had.

Sally and I had to keep reminding each other that we had made this story up out of whole cloth, and it was probably not right in every detail, or even most details, but it did not have to be. It just had to be right enough to enable us to help get the goods on Massimo. Which made me realize that, though we still had no hard evidence, I so wanted Plan B to work that I was close to convincing myself Massimo actually had done it, or at least something like it.

* * *

It's a simple gambit. Send the provocative email but

make no demand. Wait for the target's reply to formulate the next step.

The *PI Handbook* states that the most common response is some version of "Who are you?" and/or "What do you want?" Unless you're completely off base, in which case you get no reply at all or a variant of "What the fuck?"

It was getting late, and I was fried. "I think we should pack it in," I said. "We don't know how often Massimo checks his email."

* * *

Two days later and still no response from Massimo. We had to conclude that he had ignored the email. It was the act of an innocent man.

Disheartened, I was in my office after stopping at the bakery for a bag of donuts and the fro-yo shop for a couple of Rocket Smoothies to share with Sally, who arrived about ten minutes later. We needed the comfort food to boost our sagging spirits.

In my drive to exonerate Boomer, had I jumped the gun? That question had been nagging at me with increasing vigor. This wasn't a TV show where the detectives solve a complex crime in an hour, less commercial breaks, with repeated leaps of intuition and lucky coincidences. In the real world, most cases take time and patience, with a lot more plodding than sprinting, a lot more wrong turns than right ones. All of which I said to Sally as we selected from the dozen assorted.

I worked on my maple bar. Sally nibbled her chocolate glazed. It turned out I wasn't the only one who had been ruminating.

"I've been thinking," she said. "How did they identify the body?"

"You know. I told you about the necklace and that anagram stuff."

Sally nodded. "So Massimo couldn't really identify it."

I shook my head. "I saw the corpse. Believe me, there was no way to visually identify it. And they couldn't use DNA, it's unreliable when exposed to that kind of heat."

"So, if no necklace, no hard evidence, right?"

"Well, yes, but given the circumstances…"

"Right. Circumstantial. So humor me, Joe. Suppose there's no necklace, what do they do?"

"Probably try dental records. It was what they used before DNA."

Sally polished off the glazed and switched to a cinnamon twist. "Didn't you tell me Uncle Bill said the more confusing the case, the better for Boomer."

I nodded. "He said the defense should sow confusion."

"So," Sally said, "let's sow."

Chapter 14

"I am not working on Boomer's case," I said by way of greeting the next morning.

"Good thing," Ed Wax said.

"I only called to see if you have any other work that may be coming up for me."

"Because you're so busy you may have a scheduling problem?"

"My services are much in demand," I said.

"Right. So what is it?"

"Just a thought. Are you certain it was Gianni's body in the barn?"

Maybe it was just phone static, but I thought I could hear gears turning as Ed uncharacteristically hesitated before he said, "Oh, shit."

* * *

Massimo's identification based on the necklace would have been good enough for the authorities in most circumstances. But this was a felony homicide case and once Ed challenged the identification, the DA had no choice but to ask the ME to reopen the issue.

Like I had told Sally, DNA was useless in identifying a body as badly incinerated as the corpse I'd found in Boomer's barn. Even if DNA could somehow be extracted, it could too easily be damaged or contaminated under those conditions for a definitive determination. They would have to try the old-fashioned way, dental records. Which they did. Which revealed that the remains were not those of Gianni Piscatelli.

Which in and of itself did not change the charges against Boomer. Negligent homicide is negligent homicide, regardless of the identity of the victim. The now unidentified but nonetheless deceased victim.

Still, I bet the DA also said "oh, shit" when he got that report. Because it raised a lot of questions, all of which Ed Wax repeated publicly and often.

If it wasn't Gianni, who was it?

What were they doing in Gianni's RV? More, I had found the body outside the vehicle. There was no hard evidence the person had even been in the RV.

What was the person doing wearing Gianni's necklace?

Was foul play involved? It was the very question Uncle Bill had raised. If the unidentified victim was already dead or even badly injured before the fire and explosion, Boomer would be off the hook.

And déjà vu, where was Gianni?

Shaking his head in dismay, Ed Wax concluded with the defense attorney's classic refrain, "My client is the victim of sloppy police work and the DA's rush to judgement."

* * *

Plan B was over. It had done its job, but in an entirely unexpected way. It had led us to ask the right question.

Ed had his investigator turning over every possible rock and the cops were re-engaged. The charges against Boomer had not yet been dropped, but the DA's hedgy pronouncements indicated he was giving himself wiggle room. There were just too many loose ends, too much room for the defense to paint reasonable doubt all over the case in court. Just like Uncle Bill had said.

The public's renewed interest in the case quickly morphed, as the search for Gianni Piscatelli became the focus. And when inevitably his secret identity as Sir Dean Fischer leaked, the Internet went bonkers.

Everyone, it seemed, was searching for Gianni Piscatelli. Or at least posting about it.

Gianni spottings abounded.

* * *

The good news for Boomer just kept coming.

Life Is Never Easy

First came the embarrassing revelation that the medical examiner had further modified her report. It seemed a more thorough examination of the remains had revealed a fracture between C1 and C2 that had somehow previously escaped notice. Which could have killed the unidentified victim or at least contributed to his demise. It was the proverbial blunt force trauma, but how it happened was unclear. Possibly from a fall, but foul play could not be ruled out. The important thing for our side, which was how I thought about it, was that the cause of death was now listed as undetermined.

Not to be outdone in incompetence, at Ed Wax's insistence the cops examined the RV's odometer, which was still sufficiently intact to give a reading. Seems they had forgotten to do that when the recovered the VIN. It revealed that the mileage was the same as on the paperwork for the transfer of title to Gianni. Meaning that the RV had never left the barn since before Gianni purchased it.

For the beleaguered district attorney, it was the last straw. The charge of negligent homicide against Boomer was dropped.

Chapter 15

Massimo

Gianni was right. Life is never easy. In fact, I'm screwed.

It was after midnight and his family was asleep as Massimo sat on the front porch of his cousin's guest house, sipping whiskey and brooding,

How had it come to this?

* * *

It started with his secret negotiations in January and February with Grapewest to sell the albatross that was Piscatelli Vineyards. It was a sweet deal that would set Massimo and his family up for life. And just when he was trying to work out how to get his parents to sign the agreement, along came COVID and they died. Sure, that was sad, but their health, physical and mental, had been going downhill fast anyway. As their priest said, it was time for God to take them. A blessing.

Then Gianni refused to even consider the deal. Suddenly, he's mister family legacy, adamant about honoring the way-too-often-expressed wishes of their parents to keep the vineyard in the family, honor their ancestors, blah-blah-blah.

That was the last straw. Massimo had finally had it with the little freeloading fucker. Who, among other sibling sins, constantly lauded his superior command of the English language over the down to earth speech of his more practically educated brother. Never failed to remind Massimo that he had a Master of Fine Arts degree from Cal, the top school in the University of California system, whereas Massimo had what Gianni derided as little more than a trade school degree from Davis.

Massimo was flooded with a lifetime of pent-up resentment but resisted acting in the heat of the moment. Quite the opposite. After that blowup at the funeral, he seemingly made peace with Gianni. But in truth, he was just biding his time.

Meanwhile, the pandemic caused a bidding war for the upcoming Piscatelli harvest. That was a nice surprise. The business had been losing money for the last couple of years. The brokers were all assholes who could not be trusted, and Massimo had been forced to sell the last two harvests piecemeal at cut rate prices.

His father kept telling him not to deal with the brokers. Instead he should cultivate relationships with the owners of a few select wineries like his father had done and sell Piscatelli's premium grapes to them direct, and for premium prices.

* * *

Massimo refilled his glass. His sips had turned into slugs.
Didn't Dad realize I didn't have time to do relationships, I had a vineyard to run. On my own. Last thing I needed was my old man needling me all the time.

* * *

Anyway, while he was trying to figure out what to do about Gianni, the pandemic changed the game. With people staying home, demand for wine surged and the buyers were suddenly hounding him with offers. It was an irresistible lure. Massimo signed a contract locking in a premium price after confirming that Grapewest was willing to keep their deal on the table until after the 2020 harvest if he signed a letter of intent. Which he did in a heartbeat.

He would harvest and deliver the grapes in the fall for a windfall, then immediately close the Grapewest deal. Talk about having your cake and eating it too!

Life Is Never Easy

* * *

There was just one small detail. Somewhere along the way, he had to change Gianni's mind. But the more he thought about it, the more he became convinced he was fooling himself. Massimo knew his brother. Gianni was stubborn. Terminally stubborn.

After Boomer and Sarge had moved onto that yacht and then gotten infected with the virus, Boomer had told Massimo he and Sarge were unlikely to ever move back. So when Gianni told him he had bought Sarge's RV, Massimo saw his opportunity.

It was simple. They just walked over to Boomer's barn together to look at Gianni's new toy and Massimo bashed him across the back of the head from behind with a length of pipe. He channeled his Little League coach: "Swing through the ball." His coach would have been proud. One swing was all it took. Sure, crossing that line, murdering his brother had given him pause. But not enough to stop him from doing it.

He lugged Gianni's body up the ladder on the back of the RV and tossed him down on his back. It would look like Gianni had fallen backward and hit his head on the barn floor doing who knows what on that ladder. Tragic accident.

Massimo returned home, surreptitiously packed some of Gianni's things, took the suitcases to the barn and arranged the stuff in the RV. Poof. Ostensibly, Gianni had once again taken off for parts unknown, this time in his new mobile home.

Massimo left the body on the floor of the barn. No one would have a reason to go there. No one ever came up the road unless they had business at the vineyard, let alone wandered back to Boomer's barn.

He was in no rush to have the body discovered. Maybe during the harvest he would send someone over to Boomer's to borrow something from the barn. He could work out those details later.

As spring turned to summer, the body decomposed and critters did their thing, all the better to make it hard to tell exactly what had happened.

* * *

It had been kinda weird, having Gianni lying there rotting. Odd what you can get used to.

* * *

The harvest was about to get underway when a freak lightning storm ignited the devastating wildfire, actually a series of fires lit by separate strikes over a wide area of San Mateo and Santa Cruz counties. It would take over a month to contain.

As the inferno inexorably approached Piscatelli

Life Is Never Easy

Vineyards, Massimo understood that there would be no harvest, and a deal with Grapewest was highly unlikely regardless of the letter of intent. Who would buy a vineyard whose vines had been destroyed and which was now in an area that climate change had demonstrably turned into a potential future burn zone?

Massimo shook his fist at the heavens decrying this outrageous, unfair act of God, then focused on dealing with the emergency. His got his staff and family evacuated before sunset. He promised to follow them after he loaded as many valuables as he could onto his truck and took care of other unnamed last-minute chores.

Those chores consisted of restaging the scene at the barn, assuring that Boomer's chemicals would accelerate the fire, reduce the corpse to ashes and destroy the RV and its contents as well. That done, he waited out on the road in his truck as a wall of flame roared over the ridge and raced towards the barn like a tidal wave from hell, driving off to safety just as the barn exploded.

Massimo's grand scheme had been foiled on the brink of brilliant success by the vagaries of nature, but there was no time to cry over spilt milk. He engaged Boomer's PI friend to cement his alibi, knowing Gianni's remains would eventually be discovered. Then he waited to see how things played out.

* * *

Getting his friend Boomer jammed up was not part of the plan. Massimo felt bad about that. Boomer was good people. He just did not anticipate the legal problem he would cause for him. He was just getting comfortable with chalking it up as collateral damage when, out of the blue, the medical examiner declared that further investigation revealed the corpse found in Boomer's barn was not that of Gianni Piscatelli. The proof, the idiot ME declared, was from Gianni's dental records and was indisputable. Although, she added, who the deceased was remained a mystery.

Massimo learned about this incomprehensible lunacy when Detective Azevedo arrived at his door armed with tough new questions. And this time he was accompanied by his partner. Massimo told the detectives he was shocked. It was a huge understatement.

Obviously pissed at the humiliating bogus victim ID which they blamed on Massimo, they double-teamed him, played good cop/bad cop, cajoled and threatened. Azevedo was particularly interested in the necklace

"How did it get on my John Doe? You sure your brother didn't have a special friend he gave it to, then maybe they had a falling out?"

"I don't know any more than what I've already told you," Massimo said, and, despite the grilling, stuck to that line.

* * *

Life Is Never Easy

It had been easy going for dumbfounded because I was. Still am. Completely dumbfounded.

Now, with Gianni legally alive, Massimo couldn't dispose of the business assets, couldn't inherit his brother's money. He was ruined.

Worse, there was that crazy email. The one that had nearly paralyzed him with fear. The one he could not bring himself to answer.

Yep, completely screwed. And someone out there knows.

The bottle was empty, but Massimo no longer cared. The glass slipped from his hand and shattered as he passed out.

Chapter 16

"I'm a free man with nowhere to go." Boomer's wide grin, displayed on my living room TV, belied his lament.

"Sounds like a line from a country song," Sally said.

We were in my condo celebrating remotely with Boomer and Sarge. The four of us were drinking champagne. Boomer raised his glass.

"A toast to you all for your support."

We raised our glasses, then sipped.

"Some mystery, huh?" Boomer said. "Somebody should write a book about it. Maybe make it into a movie, like that one about the case when we first worked together, Joe. The thing where Rex Baker got himself blown up on his TV show. What was it called again?"

"The TV show was *Venture Capital Pie,*" Sally said. "Baker called himself Mr. Perfect, so they called the movie *Perfect Murder*."

"Sure wonder who the dude in my barn was," Boomer said. "And where the hell Gianni is at."

Life Is Never Easy

* * *

After the guys signed off, Sally and I ordered dinner from Lasagna, Lasagna. While we waited for the food to arrive, we worked on finishing the champagne.

Sally said, "You gonna tell me what you did?"

"I ordered dinner," I said. Mr. Innocent.

Sally gave me that glare that said, *You can't bullshit me!* "For starters, you did not write that Hawaii thing."

"If I recall correctly, I never exactly said I did, did I?" I had been careful about not outright lying to her. "Trust me, I can't tell you who did."

I had promised Cora Mott I would keep it a secret between the two of us when I enlisted her help to snare Massimo, whom she despised. In exchange, she promised not to reveal what I had told her, which pretty much amounted to our Plan B story at the time.

Sally sighed. "I trust you, Joe. I even believe you. What about the dental records?"

"How did you know?"

"You committed to finding Gianni, but you gave up the search too easily. Not like you, even after you're off the case. Tells me you did find him. Dead. Not like we figured in Plan B; we got the timing wrong. But not the motive. Or the killer. But it always came back to the same problem: how to prove Massimo did it? We couldn't. No hard evidence. So you decided to get some justice for Gianni regardless."

It was my turn to sigh. "Dental records are all electronic. I happen to know a couple of guys who could mess with them."

"Like Jonathan and Charles," Sally said. "But you're not saying."

But I was smiling.

"What convinced you Massimo killed Gianni?"

"The odometer. It meant it didn't happen like we thought in Plan B. After he bought the RV, it had never moved. Yet Massimo said Gianni planned to take off in it. It was one of several things he had somehow forgotten to tell me when he hired me to supposedly find his brother. Which I realized was a coverup. For someone desperate to locate Gianni, he was remarkably uncooperative. He was just using me to build an alibi."

"He killed Gianni and left him in the barn," Sally said with a shudder. "How gruesome."

"And now he can't get Gianni's money or salvage the business," I said.

"He sure is screwed," Sally said, raising her glass.

"That he is," I said as we clinked.

Retirement Plan

Prologue

spring 2020

Alejandro Zapatero sat beside the pool at his walled estate—he thought of it as his country retreat—in a wealthy suburb of the resort Dominican city of Punta Cana, took a long pull on his beer, and smiled.

The bikini clad woman on the chaise lounge several feet away from him returned his smile and sipped her fruity cold drink.

They were alone at the estate, except, of course, for the servants and bodyguards who blended into the background like furnishings. Zapato liked privacy.

He sighed. He also liked looking at the woman's body, the fine scars that accented her curves. But he would keep his distance. No sense taking unnecessary chances. Zapato was bold, but he was not reckless.

"How are you feeling?" he said.

"Thanks to the priest's warning and the excellent care you arranged for me at this very private health spa,

I'm fully recovered."

Zapato nodded. "That is good to hear."

They enjoyed a few quiet moments, broken only by the sounds of birdsong.

"You are sure she bought it?" he said.

"Every bit of it," she said. "Everything from my supposed mental illness to my suicidal thoughts to my guilt-ridden remorse."

"And you are certain you can impersonate her?"

"Perhaps not to someone who knows her well, but otherwise, perfectly. As soon as my hair grows out. We look almost like twins. Our voices sound alike. I know her mannerisms and history. And you have the copies I made of her driver's license and passport."

"Yes, our forger is working on them."

"And the fingerprints and DNA were satisfactory?"

"I'm told the quality was excellent. Your training in forensics has served us well."

She studied Zapato's face. As always, she found herself unable to read him. "When do we make our move?"

"Not yet. My focus is elsewhere. The opportunity to expand our operations to the West Coast came sooner than expected. Not only did Rick Varga do us the favor of drowning, his entire organization has now been dismantled. So enjoy yourself here until I tell you it is your time."

They again lapsed into silence. Then she found the need to stretch her arms towards the sun and roll onto her side so her breasts were aimed at him like headlights. She smiled coyly as his eyes took her in, sensing his desire. "As you wish."

Zapato rose. "Now, I am afraid I must leave you."

As he strode away, Angie Brown rolled back onto her back, pulled her broad-brimmed hat over her face, and smiled broadly. She would happily bide her time in this tropical paradise.

Thank you, dear sister.

Chapter 1

6 months later

Jennifer Perez could not recall ever feeling so bone-weary. Weeks of double shifts, dealing with the constant pressure of treating COVID patients in the overcrowded, understaffed hospital, the constant threat of exposure, had ground her down.

Her trek through the poorly lit staff parking lot was made more miserable by the cold rain that had come on unexpectedly off Lake Michigan that evening. More so because she had no umbrella, no head covering whatsoever, and only a thin and now soaking wet cardigan.

As she headed to her car just before midnight, all Jennifer could think about was getting out of her soggy clothes, enjoying a glass of wine, and crawling into bed next to her husband. And the blessing of sleep.

Retirement Plan

* * *

Jennifer's body was found next to her car by a coworker minutes after her assailant fled into the darkness. Her diamond ring and wallet were missing. The police chalked it up to a mugging gone bad, just another addict desperate for a fix, whose knife had fatally penetrated the victim's heart as she desperately, though foolishly, fought back.

They got that last bit wrong. Jennifer was no fool. She had willingly parted with her valuables. Still, she had been murdered.

They got most of the rest right. He was a druggie with a long record of petty theft and minor drug offenses. His body was discovered a few hours later next to a dumpster in a nearby alley, the needle with the fentanyl-laced heroin still in his arm, the knife with his victim's blood and his fingerprints on it under his corpse. Case closed.

* * *

The rapid police work was no solace to distraught Jean-Paul Perez. He and Jennifer had been together for three decades and were about to celebrate their 25th wedding anniversary. Childless, him an orphan, her shunned by a family that could not accept their interracial marriage, they were devoted to each other. Jennifer had been his world. Now, without warning, she was gone.

By nature shy and reclusive, a bereft Jean-Paul withdrew not only from the outside world, aided by the isolation inherent in dealing with the pandemic, but from his feelings as well, robotically delivering the mail for the U.S. Postal Service. It was a job he could perform in protective isolation, returning to his modest home each evening to stare mindlessly at the TV screen.

* * *

A little over a week after Jennifer's death, the doorbell rang. Annoyed—it was dinner time, though he was only beginning to think, without enthusiasm, about what to prepare—Jean-Paul opened the front door.

It occurred to Jean-Paul that he could only guess what the woman who stood on his front porch looked like behind the requisite mask she was wearing. Which reminded him he wasn't wearing one. He took a social distancing step back. "Can I help you?"

Jean-Paul watched as several emotions seemed to flash like a slide show in the woman's big brown eyes. "There's really no way to ease into this, Mr. Perez. My name is Sally Rocket. I'm your daughter."

Chapter 2

Seated in the living room, she waited while Jean-Paul quickly fetched a mask. He positioned himself across the coffee table from his utterly unexpected guest. She told Jean-Paul that she knew his wife had recently died and extended her condolences.

As was his habit when bewildered, Jean-Paul sought the shelter of playing a role, in this case that of the courteous host. He offered his guest a beverage. She politely declined. He noted the time and asked if she was in need of dinner. After a bit of discussion, he ordered pizza. Having run out of avoidance tactics, Jean-Paul prompted her to explain herself.

During the pandemic lockdown, she said, she had decided to use the enforced time home alone to search for her biological father. As a small child, she had learned from overhearing her parents fighting that Emmanuel Roquette, the man she called Daddy, was not her biological father. He had married her pregnant mother just before fleeing the chaos and atrocities of their native Haiti after the 1991 military coup that ousted Jean Bertrand Aristide, Haiti's first democratically elected leader. Roquette had wagered that a married man with a pregnant wife would be treated sympathetically by American immigration authorities. He bet correctly. After spending time in a refugee camp at Guantanamo, the young couple was admitted to the United States where Sally was born.

Her mother eventually left home, never to return, she said, and when she was ten years old, her father, too, abandoned her. Sally became a ward of the state, alone in the world. Somehow, in that bureaucratic process, Roquette became Rocket.

As she told her tale, Jean-Paul became increasingly distracted. Now he interrupted her narrative.

"Her name," he said softly. "What was your mother's name?"

"Her name was Farah," she said. "I don't know her maiden name."

Jean-Paul nodded slowly. Almost in a whisper, he said, "Yes, I remember a girl named Farah. But it was so long ago..."

The pizza arrived. Jean-Paul opened a bottle of red wine, and their masks came off. They ate in silence, Jean-Paul deep in thought. She gave him space to gather his thoughts. After finishing his second slice, he said, "I am from Haiti. I was there during that terrible time. But what makes you think I'm your father?"

And you just happened to remember a young

Retirement Plan

woman name Farah, she thought. *Excellent.* She reached into her handbag and took out a couple of sheets of paper stapled together. "It was this genealogy website. When I decided to look for you, I submitted my DNA to a few of them. Then this one came up with a hit." She handed the report across the coffee table to Jean-Paul.

He read it slowly and with great care. There were lots of numbers and scientific mumbo-jumbo, but the conclusion was unambiguous. They had matched Sally Rocket's DNA to another client's, who most certainly was her biological father.

"This doesn't say who that client is," Jean-Paul said, carefully laying the report on the table.

"No, they're big on privacy. How they work is that they put me in touch with the client through their app. That turned out to be your wife. She told me she had submitted your DNA without you knowing, hoping to discover if by some chance you had any relatives in the United States. Something about an anniversary surprise, a gift of some sort. Anyway, she said she had not expected to discover you had a child. That seemed to be more of a surprise than she had counted on. She said she would have to think about it and get back to me. Then she went silent. But her messages had given me some clues. I did some digging around online, found out she had died, dug some more, and here I am."

"That was pretty good digging," Jean-Paul said.

"I live in Silicon Valley and have techy friends," she said, waving her hand as if that of course explained everything. Which, to technophobic Jean-Paul, to whom such things were akin to magic, it did.

Jean-Paul took a deep breath that amounted to more of a deep sigh. He stared at her and said, "Daughter?"

Angie Brown, the woman calling herself Sally Rocket, nodded, reached across the table, touched his hand, and smiled. "Father."

It was not a question.

And sometime in the ensuing few days, he began calling her "my gift."

* * *

A week later, Jean-Paul turned in his papers, retiring after over two decades working for the United States Postal Service. The rumor at the post office was that his wife's murder had triggered a serious heart condition, and that his newly discovered daughter would be caring for him, though no one could say for certain how that rumor had started. There was also an unconfirmed report that he had contracted a severe case of the virus.

What was certain was that his house was put on the market and the moving van arrived even before it sold. But the van had a short trip, to a Chicago warehouse that specialized in estate liquidation.

Retirement Plan

Jean-Paul's forwarding address was in the village of Keokea on Maui. Had he lived closer to where he had worked, this would have been the source of considerable excitement for his erstwhile colleagues. But his local post office was across town from his former workplace and his change of address form drew no undue attention.

Chapter 3

As soon as Angie had been old enough to understand, her mother began telling her about her father. Jill Brown at first simply explained that she had left her husband when she learned she was expecting Angie because he was a bad man. As time passed, like a sculptor working with clay, layers of nuance were added.

By the time Angie was 16, she understood it all. Emmanuel Roquette was a conman who only cared about people if they could help him rip off other people. He had married her mother because her pregnancy had helped get him out of Haiti and into the United States. "He had no other use for me, except for sex and then taking care of your sister." Angie knew her sister had been only two years old when her mother left. By then, her father was already using her sister to lure his marks into parting with their money. It was not a life Angie's mom wanted for herself or the baby growing inside her.

She had wanted to take Sally—that was her sister's name—with her when she left, but the little girl was completely under her fiercely controlling father's spell

Retirement Plan

and had increasingly less use for her mother. Farah Roquette—she had long ago told Angie about changing her name to Jill Brown to help hide from the bastard—decided she had to leave Sally behind, a decision she regretted until the day she died.

Jill Brown worked two jobs to support herself and her daughter. By day, she cleaned homes in affluent Richmond, Virginia neighborhoods. At night, she cleaned the downtown offices in which the professionals who lived in those neighborhoods worked. Angie and her mom lived in a rough neighborhood, but Richmond had much worse, and their tiny home was always clean and tidy. Jill lived frugally, rode the bus to and from work, and made sure Angie was as well taken care of as possible.

Angie was used to being on her own. For as long as she could remember, she had taken care of herself during the week, especially after school. Summers, she went to a day camp for disadvantaged, urban children; it was oversubscribed, but her mom had somehow gotten her in. As a teenager, her mother had only a few rules for her daughter: get good grades and graduate; stay out of jail; don't get pregnant. Angie took all three admonitions to heart.

* * *

It happened on an overcast November night, when the

sun set early. Angie, then a sophomore in high school, was letting herself into the house after visiting a friend after school, when the man, high on a concoction of illicit drugs, came up behind her, seemingly out of nowhere, pushed her inside, and locked the door. Angie was overpowered and nearly knocked unconscious. Her mother, catching a few hours of sleep before heading to her night job, was awakened and rushed downstairs, but was no match for their attacker.

An hour later, both women had been beaten, raped, stabbed repeatedly, and left for dead. Somehow, Angie managed to get to the phone and call 9-1-1. Before the EMTs arrived, Jill whispered her last words to her badly injured daughter. Then she died in her arms.

Though it was touch and go for over a week, Angie survived. But her body was covered with scars, her reproductive organs damaged beyond repair. As was her psyche. Although she looked fine in clothes, and her face was unmarked, she found her disfigured nakedness repulsive. And she could never have a child. Angie was certain that no man would ever want her.

* * *

They caught the animal. It was a short trial. Angie's account, including her identification of their assailant, was unshakable during cross-examination. That, and the evidence provided by the crime scene investigator, led to a quick guilty verdict on all charges, including first-degree murder, attempted murder and two counts of rape.

Two things happened during that trial that changed Angie's life. First, she was in awe of the evidence provided by the CSI. Fingerprints, DNA, and fibers helped lead the police to the perpetrator, and the CSI's calm, authoritative testimony left no doubt that the accused had committed the horrific crime for which he stood accused.

Angie Brown had found her vocation.

She also had an epiphany. The reason her mother had worked herself to the bone to support them, the reason they had lived in crime- and drug-infested neighborhoods, the reason she was now alone in the world, was Emmanuel Roquette. How different their lives would have been with a decent man as husband and father to provide for them and protect them. To the end, her mother had sacrificed herself for Angie. She vowed that she would repay her. However long it took, she would exact retribution on Emmanuel Roquette.

Because she could not get her mother's last gasp from intruding in her thoughts at seemingly random times: *This is all his fault.*

Angie Brown had found her purpose.

* * *

After she graduated from college, loaded with student debt, Angie returned to Richmond to start work as an entry level forensic lab tech. Her work ethic and skills led to rapid promotion to criminalist, working in the field and in the lab to perform crime scene investigation and evidence analysis.

Angie devoted nearly every spare moment to the hunt for Emmanuel Roquette. It had been frustrating, seemingly futile work, until she managed to get herself attached to the local anti-terrorism task force. Low on the totem pole though she was, this gave her access to a wide range of investigative resources.

She confirmed her mom's narrative, tracking Emmanuel Roquette from the Haitian refugee camp at Guantanamo to his entry into the United States in Louisiana in 1992. There was little else until he renewed his driver's license in 2000. Then, nothing. Shortly after the turn of the century, Emmanuel Roquette had either died or changed his identity. Angie chose to believe the latter.

You didn't have to be a CSI to know that you can change your name, even alter your appearance, but fingerprints don't lie. So it was that Angie Brown swiped her parents' files from the internment records buried in a federal warehouse coincidentally but conveniently located close to her home in Richmond, Virginia. The files didn't contain much new information, but she did

Retirement Plan

obtain fingerprint cards and photos of Farah and Emmanuel Roquette. The files confirmed her mother's pregnancy with her sister. Angie was also struck by how much younger and vibrant her mother looked in that photo. As far back as Angie could remember, her mom had looked old and haggard.

Using her taskforce credentials, Angie ran her father's fingerprints through IAFIS, the national fingerprint database used by law enforcement and run by the FBI, along with other databases with more restricted access. A few close matches, but none of a Black male in a reasonable age range.

Once a month thereafter, Angie ran the same query against all fingerprints newly added to this vast repository, with the same negative result. Her patience was rewarded when the Nevada Gaming Commission added the fingerprints of one John Wilson, a new casino employee; all casino staff were printed as part of a mandatory background-check. That led to Wilson's gaming commission file. It contained a photo, which looked surprisingly like her father's 1992 picture. Unlike her mother, her father had aged well.

Angie immediately put in for vacation. She flew to Vegas. Stayed in a dumpy motel on the outskirts of Sin City. The only weapon she carried was the camera on her phone.

She tracked down John Wilson, working in a casino

on the Strip. Tailed him for a couple of days. Discovered he was also using the name James Johnson. One morning, she found he had checked out of his long-term motel and was gone.

She returned home and eventually picked up the trail again. He was using the James Johnson alias. It wasn't like he had been trying to hide. His credit card transactions on a company card for an outfit named Jacmel Enterprises placed him in someplace called Los Gatos, California, which turned out to be an upscale suburb of San Jose. *Who the hell names a town The Cats?*

Angie once more put in for vacation.

Chapter 4

It was time for revenge.

Angie Brown headed west. She located her father and, to cause him pain, murdered his girlfriend. By sheer chance, in tribute to the gods of coincidence, Sally Rocket, the sister their mother had abandoned all those years before, became a suspect in the crime, in large part because the two women looked so much alike.

When the dust cleared, Sally was exonerated, Emmanuel Roquette was in jail for life, successfully framed by Angie for yet another cold-blooded murder she had committed.

Angie, wanted for the first killing, was hiding in the Dominican Republic, using the name Angela Sanchez, where she met the man known as Zapato. And where she spent a week at the start of the COVID pandemic meeting clandestinely with her newfound older sister.

The women bonded and shared their stories. During which Sally revealed that she had not known that Emmanuel Roquette was not her biological father before recent events, and that she still did not know the identity of her real father. For her part, Angie withheld the fact that her mother had long ago told her Sally's father's name. And a bit more.

* * *

In 1991, Jean-Paul Perez was a teenage baseball phenom in a country whose interest in baseball was manufacturing them. Taking advantage of dirt-cheap labor, American companies had built factories that supplied Haitian baseballs to the world.

Haiti, one of the poorest countries on the planet, shares the island of Hispaniola with its comparatively prosperous eastern neighbor the Dominican Republic, whose interest in baseball was playing the game and exporting its best players to America.

After a military coup overthrew the Aristide government, young Jean-Paul slipped across the border. He leveraged his athletic prowess to bypass immigration restrictions and was soon playing for one of the baseball-mad Dominican Republic's top teams, where he drew the attention of American major league scouts. A year later, he was playing for a minor league team in Texas, a gifted shortstop with a rifle arm, destined for the Big Show. Meanwhile, his major league sponsors deftly shepherded him through the U.S. immigration process, as they had many other Latin American and

Retirement Plan

Caribbean players.

It was during spring training for the season in which he was considered a shoo-in for a major league roster spot that Jean-Paul blew out his shoulder. Though he spent a couple of more years rattling around the minors, he was never the same.

One good thing resulted from Jean-Paul's injury. During the course of his rehabilitation, he met a young nurse name Jennifer who eventually became his wife. By which time Jean-Paul had secured a coveted green card that led, in due course, to his becoming an American citizen.

* * *

Angie's mother had told her that Sally's father had been a star teenage baseball player all the girls in her neighborhood were in love with. But Farah knew nothing about what had happened to Jean-Paul Perez after she left Haiti.

Alejandro Zapatero's organization was responsible for a major portion of the drugs smuggled into the United States and he had a vast and far-flung network. Armed with Angie's information, albeit decades old, he had little trouble locating Jean-Paul Perez.

It was the missing piece of his retirement plan.

Chapter 5

The second heart attack had been decisive.

The prognosis and treatment plan were clear. He could live a long life if he took his medication, watched his diet, and got proper exercise. Oh yes, and one more thing. He had to reduce his stress. Because the next one would in all likelihood be fatal.

Which presented a quandary. Constant high stress was not an option in Zapato's business. Nor was there a retirement plan, an off-ramp for the leader of an enterprise such as his. His peers who tried to exit from the pinnacle of power or even just tried to slow down did not long survive in the cutthroat competition to supplant the leader. If not murdered outright, the constant anxiety of living with extreme personal security protection, unable to trust anyone, protectors included, led to an early grave.

No matter that he had stashed away an immense fortune. Living to enjoy it was not in the cards. Unless...

* * *

Retirement Plan

Alejandro Zapatero, head of the Dominican drug cartel, approached this dilemma as he had so many other immense challenges he had faced as he had clawed his way to the pinnacle of power. His proven formula was based on careful planning and preparation coupled with ruthless tactics and decisive action.

At the age of 13, the youngest of five children, Zapato left his impoverished family that was led by a single mother, never to return. He emerged from the mean streets of Santo Domingo a ruthless, self-reliant, self-contained survivor. It was during that time that he acquired his nickname, Zapato. In Spanish, shoe. Or, in his case, The Boot, the man who put his foot on your neck and kept it there until he got what he wanted. Or you perished.

Having intentionally lost touch with his family, he had been careful to form no romantic entanglements, nothing like a close relationship. Nor had he any children of which he was aware. All of which he believed had been an asset in his profession; such things were an unnecessary distraction and made you vulnerable. This lack of personal attachments certainly simplified his disappearing act.

That his plan called for the deaths of two innocents—and one not-so innocent—did not at all faze him. He gave it not a moment's consideration. Causing death, directly or indirectly, had long been a routine part of his life.

In truth, the only life that mattered to Zapato was his own.

* * *

Just after midnight, Zapato slipped out of his Punta Cana compound. An hour later, in the guise of a fisherman, he trudged onto the docks, boarded a humble fishing boat, and was soon headed east into the Mono passage, in the direction of Puerto Rico. Alone.

Three days later, also in the middle of the night, he stripped and let the boat drift away as he swam to shore. There, he removed clothing from the waterproof bag he had toted on his back and headed off on foot towards San Juan.

The next morning, having spent the night in a cheap motel on the outskirts of the city, the man whose driver's license now identified him as Douglas Jones from Miami took a taxi to the airport and caught the first flight, ostensibly home.

Three hours later, Mr. Jones rented a car, parked in the short-term lot, and checked into the Miami International Airport Hotel. In his room, he shaved off the beard he had worn since he was in his late teens. The face of the man who stared back at him from the mirror looked shockingly unfamiliar.

Which made him smile.

Retirement Plan

He spent the next couple of hours doing some shopping in the terminal, whose shops offered everything from clothing to toiletries to cell phones. After lunch at an airport restaurant, he began the long drive north. He had a date in two days with Angie Brown. They had a liquidation to attend to.

* * *

What they thought of as the weakest link in the plan turned out not to be. Jean-Paul had been duly curious about Sally and her motives, but he was not by nature suspicious. He pretty much accepted her and her well-rehearsed explanations at face value. He had probed a bit, yes, but done little to verify checkable facts about the person called Sally Rocket. To the superficial extent he did, all had checked out to his satisfaction. She was as she claimed, an unmarried self-defense instructor from California, where she seemed to have led an ordinary adult life.

She chalked this up to her charm and her mark's utter ineptitude with technology. Zapato, who believed you made your own luck, attributed it to meticulous preparation. They had contingency plans ready if Jean-Paul found a reason to question Angie's identity. Happily, they had not needed to use them.

Regardless, all that was now behind them.

Chapter 6

Keokea is in Maui's rugged, sparsely populated upcountry on the western slopes of Haleakala, the volcano which formed most of the island. At an elevation of nearly 3,000 feet with many spectacular views of the crowded beaches from Maalaea to Wailea, as well as the islands of Lanai and Kahoolawe, the up country is a rugged land of scattered farms and ranches, with a smattering of nearby, rustic tourist attractions for those staying at the lowland resorts that include a botanical garden, goat farm, and the island's only winery.

The older man and thirtyish woman moved into the gated ranch without fanfare, having carefully navigated Hawaii's complex of pandemic regulations for arriving travelers. Locals took note that they were Black, a rarity in the area. And he did have a bit of an accent, though they could not quite place it, a tribute to the many hours he had spent watching American movies, practicing both the language and pronunciation. In any case, their new neighbors cared little about such things.

It was said that the gentleman was retired and in

poor health, the woman was his caregiver and likely bed partner, and they lived off his investments and pension, though the funding for the former and source of the latter were unknown.

In truth, few in the rural community, with its tradition of live-and-let-live libertarianism and respect for privacy, were particularly curious about the newcomers who kept to themselves and scrupulously observed pandemic precautions. The folks who lived in the area were primarily focused on survival, as ranching and farming became increasingly impacted by climate change and the tourism-based economy of their state slowly circled the drain. As was required of those who lived in vacation destinations worldwide, they bitched about the tourists all the time, right up until they stopped coming. As far as most were concerned, the much-touted vaccines under development could not come soon enough.

* * *

It had been surprisingly easy for Zapato to vanish. Other than Angie, no one knew of his plan. Nor had he left breadcrumbs behind. Most of his money had long been secretly stashed away in several banks in various countries where a premium was put on client privacy and confidentiality. The few items he and Angie could not personally handle, mainly forged documents for her, were done as part of routine cartel business. There was the elimination of Jennifer Perez and her murderer, but that was just another assignment that had trickled down the chain of command of his drug distribution empire. Nothing exceptional, nothing anyone would take note of.

Killing Jean-Paul and disposing of his body was one of the chores he and Angie had dealt with themselves. No big deal.

The plastic surgery Zapato had undergone to make him look more like Jean-Paul's driver's license photo before they flew to Hawaii could have left a trail, but the clinic had conveniently burned to the ground when a gas leak caused an explosion the night after he was discharged from care, its records destroyed.

That cosmetic procedure had been essential. It not only further disguised him from anyone who had known him in his past life, he was adamant that he himself must have no forged documents. Now Jean-Paul's Michigan driver's license looked remarkably like the clean-shaven Zapato, and he would soon trade it in for a genuine Hawaii license that would sport a photograph of his new face. Along with the banker's box of Jean-Paul's files they had brought with them, he would then have all the documentation he would need to live out his life in this tropical paradise as Jean-Paul Perez. He had not merely obtained a new identity; he had taken over that of another man. A quiet man with no

Retirement Plan

messy connections. That was the key to his plan.

As for Angie, she had arrived in Maui as Mary Williams, the remarkably common American name intentionally chosen so that anyone looking her up would face countless thousands of hits. She had the sort of vague background young people at the low end of the economic scale so often have. Most importantly, she was armed with a Hawaii driver's license and other perfectly forged paperwork to prove her new identity.

She had previously let her hair grow out to shoulder length to impersonate her sister. Before leaving the mainland with Zapato, she went back to the short, frizzy style she had used when she was hiding out in the Dominican Republic, but this time blond instead of auburn. Like Angelina Brown and Angela Sanchez, her Sally Rocket identity was but a memory.

Zapato had decided that they would forgo new passports. He did not want to risk dealing with the federal government's scrutiny. Besides, the whole point of this phase of the plan was to get them *into* the United States and establish themselves as American citizens with new, bullet-proof identities. Leaving Hawaii, let alone the United States, was not in the cards.

* * *

Jean-Paul knew that, should his enemies locate him, he was as good as dead. Still, his life experience made him more concerned about personal security than most people, a trait of which he was aware. Thus, while he had a top-drawer home security system installed at Rancho Perez, he made sure it was not so extreme as to be the subject of gossip.

The same considerations applied to guns. On the isolated farms and ranches of the upcountry, critter control combined with the distance from help in an emergency made having one or more weapons routine. He gradually acquired a few, along with the necessary permits, but neither their type nor number would attract undue attention.

* * *

She stormed into the living room, where Jean-Paul was reading a magazine. "Why are you ignoring me? I need your help with the groceries."

He looked up innocently. "I heard you calling something. I thought you were looking for a shoe."

Zapato! "Oh, shit, I did it again. I'm sorry. At least no one else heard me."

His look turned fierce, his voice, angry, as he slammed the magazine down. "That does not matter! This is no game! You must have discipline!"

He *was* Jean-Paul Perez. She *was* Mary Williams. Their former names were forbidden. Even with each other. They could not afford to screw up. No one else

Retirement Plan

could know about their prior identities, not even suspect anything might be suspicious.

He did not want to have to perform any more liquidations. In truth, he had grown quite fond of Mary and Jean-Paul Perez wanted no drama in his new life.

Chapter 7

For years, Jean-Paul had had access to a seemingly unending supply of willing women of whatever age and description he desired. Now, without that on-demand resource and given his unwillingness to risk outside liaisons, lust and proximity led to the inevitable. Though Mary thought her scars made her body ugly, he hardly noticed them, and while he had in the past resisted yielding to his desire for her, wanting no complications to interfere with her playing her part in his plan, the couple now found themselves sleeping together. And then some.

Sex notwithstanding, the power in the relationship was decidedly unbalanced. Mary was dependent on Jean-Paul, who had years of sophisticated experience hiding and controlling access to his wealth and was not inclined to allow Mary to have even the slightest information about it. On the other hand, Mary was replaceable and knew it.

Which was how Jean-Paul wanted it.

Retirement Plan

* * *

They were eating lunch on the back deck. The view of the vast cobalt ocean defined breathtaking. But it was always there, and, from their 3,000-foot-high vantage point, seemingly unchanging.

"I want to go with you to the appointment," Mary said.

Several months had passed since their arrival in the islands. They had been vaccinated and, no longer so fearful of the virus, Jean-Paul decided it was time for him to place himself in the care of a cardiologist.

But not just any cardiologist. Jean-Paul insisted on a doctor affiliated with the best hospital in the islands, Queen's Medical Center in Honolulu. It took three tries before he found one who would take him on as a patient and had a big enough ego that he did not insist on getting records from his previous cardiologist. All the man wanted to know was Jean-Paul's self-reported medical history and what meds he was taking. He would take it from there. Tomorrow, Jean-Paul would have his intake appointment.

He raised an eyebrow in surprise. "Really?"

"Yes," Mary said. "I care about you."

Jean-Paul shrugged. "Suit yourself."

Mary sipped her iced tea. "I want to see the doctor with you. You're an old man who needs his younger partner present to help with communication and his memory."

Jean-Paul looked her in the eyes for a long moment. "Excellent," he said. "You are fully into your role."

Mary looked away. The truth was that she wanted to be there because she did not trust Jean-Paul to accurately report the results of his examination.

Jean-Paul understood what was really going on. Fostering dependence was how he had created loyalty in others in the past and this situation was no different. Mary's interest in his health, he believed, was because she was dependent on him.

He was correct.

* * *

The flight from Maui's Kahului Airport to Honolulu was a quick 30-minute up-and-downer. A short taxi ride took them to the Physician's Office Building complex adjacent to Queen's Medical Center.

They were there for several hours. Jean-Paul not only received a thorough exam, he got a full lab workup and a return appointment with a primary care physician who was part of the group.

The cardiologist said everything seemed fine, pending, of course, those lab results. He wrote prescriptions to continue Jean-Paul's medication regime and gave him a pamphlet of instructions about life-style issues like diet and exercise, along with what was obviously an oft-repeated lecture that echoed the pamphlet.

They settled in for the quick return flight. "So you should be fine if you continue to behave yourself," Mary said. "You're doing well following your diet and limiting alcohol. You need to get more exercise, but don't overdo it. And check your blood pressure regularly."

Sounds like a wife, Jean-Paul thought. "I think I'm at least as interested in my health as you are. You may recall that's how we got here."

Chapter 8

They were both increasingly bored.

They had driven all over the island. Maui was beautiful, with a varied landscape from sandy beaches to rugged cliffs to rainforests to volcanic peaks. But, in truth, it was a small island, and with everything pretty much still closed due to the pandemic, and neither of them being particularly outdoorsy, they had exhausted their appetite for site-seeing drives.

They needed resorts and restaurants. Mary had always teetered on the edge of poverty. Now, with a credit card backed by her generous benefactor, much to her surprise she found she yearned to go shopping. Maui had a wide variety of upscale shops for its tourists; Mary could not wait for them to reopen. But despite the increasing pace of vaccinations, Hawaii remained COVID-wary. Things would not open up so fast.

Jean-Paul, too, was increasingly antsy. For the first time in his life, there was nothing much he had to do each day. He had gone from living at full speed for as long as he could remember to lazing in the sun day after day. He had no hobbies and now no longer in the drug-smuggling business, no interests. He found himself yearning to know how his former business was doing, particularly the West Coast expansion he had launched and the battle for power within the cartel to fill the vacuum his disappearance created. But there was no drug cartel cable channel or online news site or any other way to learn what was going on without contacting someone from his past life. That would be a foolish move, a suicidal act he forbade himself to even contemplate. The risk of exposure was too great. He constantly reminded himself: *a clean break.*

As long as I don't go out of my mind.

* * *

A tropical rainstorm became a treat, if only because it broke the monotony.

It was called island fever, a numb, claustrophobic malaise that set in as you felt yourself isolated in the middle of a seemingly endless ocean, far from any mainland and the rest of civilization, with little change in the fine weather and little motivation to do...anything much.

Jean-Paul understood that this is what all high-powered, wealthy men face in retirement. He also knew his need for isolation could only exacerbate it. But between running his business and secretly preparing to vanish without a trace, he'd had no bandwidth to prepare for this aspect of his retirement. Now it was here, unavoidable, and understanding his ennui and dealing with it were entirely different things.

And with no other outlets, he and Mary were increasingly getting on each other's nerves.

Something had to change.

* * *

It was called a ranch instead of a farm because the terrain was unsuitable for fields of crops but could support herds of livestock. Except there was no livestock.

The altitude turned the tropical climate of the Maui lowlands into a temperate one upcountry, but, despite periodic drenching downpours, drought was a growing problem. Livestock needed to graze and drink water, both of which require rainfall. Which had become increasingly unreliable. Still, most upcountry cattle ranches hung on, though with ever smaller herds.

Not so for Rancho Perez which was currently a ranch in name only. But it had once been a working cattle ranch and had kept horses to work the herd. The barn, stables, corral, and paddock, neglected though they had been for some time, were still intact.

Jean-Paul had no interest in cattle. But horses...

Retirement Plan

* * *

"Mary, meet Tommy Kamaka. Tommy's going to help me with the repairs. You know, my exercise project."

The nut-brown man with the shiny shaved head who stood next to Jean-Paul in the foyer was Mary's height, five feet, six inches, but looked to weigh a good ten pounds less than her 145. Mary took him to be in his 50s. He extended a calloused hand at the end of a well-muscled arm. His handshake was firm but comfortable, and he made good eye contact and smiled pleasantly.

"Pleased to meet you, Ms. Perez."

"My pleasure," Mary said. "I assume you're from around here."

"Yes, ma'am. All my life. Live in Kihei."

"Tommy's retired," Jean-Paul said. "He used to work for one of the big ranches. Retired after COVID hit. I convinced him to help me out part-time."

"So you're a Hawaiian cowboy?"

"You could call me that. And rest assured, I am fully vaccinated."

"Well, Mr. Cowboy, you keep an eye on this old man. Keep him from hurting himself out there."

"I'll do that," Tommy said.

* * *

Tommy's niece Lani owned a ranch that catered to tourists, providing horseback riding lessons, day trips for adults and a day camp for kids. But no tourists, no business. So she had plenty of time to teach Mary, who had never been on a horse, how to ride. And when the restoration of the ranching facilities at Rancho Perez had sufficiently progressed, Lani and Tommy helped Mary and Jean-Paul buy their own horses, one for each of them, a third for Tommy's use.

Much to his surprise, Jean-Paul enjoyed being a rancher. Even after the major rehab projects were completed, there was always something to do, from mending a fence to maintaining and repairing equipment to purchasing supplies. For her part, Mary took to caring for the horses. It was all new to her; she had never so much as had a pet before. She found that she enjoyed tending to the animals' feeding, grooming and other needs. Even mucking out the stables.

And Tommy was always there to help.

*　*　*

Unlike the dilapidated ranching facilities, the spacious residence had recently been remodeled. Which made Mary's shortcomings as a housekeeper all the more apparent. And, while she had prepared her own meals most of her life, Jean-Paul found her culinary skills sorely lacking.

Retirement Plan

Meanwhile, Mary wanted more time to ride and care for the horses.

Jean-Paul had lived in a world where cheap household help was abundantly available, and even those who were moderately well-off employed a housekeeper who often also served as the cook. He, who was far more than moderately well off, had become accustomed to having servants who were part of the household's background yet indispensable. And, as time passed and they fully settled into their new roles, Jean-Paul's concerns about keeping their secrets diminished. If Mary needed help, so be it. So long as she kept the household running smoothly, properly a woman's role, he was happy.

* * *

In the new year, Tommy's sister-in-law, Rosie, a widow with adult children, began coming every weekday, arriving in time to prepare lunch, and leaving when cleanup from dinner was completed. She quickly and firmly took charge of the household—she met no resistance doing so—with an unobtrusive, gentle manner that pleased both Mary and Jean-Paul.

* * *

They were finishing breakfast. Having sent Rosie out

on an errand, Mary reached over to the large bowl in the center of the table that Rosie kept well-stocked with a variety of fruits. She took a lemon and a lime and placed them between herself and Jean-Paul, who watched her with a puzzled expression. Saying nothing, she waited.

Jean-Paul closed his eyes and shook his head. "I did it again, didn't I?"

"You did. Last night when Rosie served the fish with sliced lemons."

This tiny detail had flummoxed Jean-Paul. He at times called lemons limes and vice-versa. In the Dominican Republic, lemons and limes were both referred to as *limóns,* though if you had to differentiate you would call a lemon a *limón amarillo.*

Mary left it at that. She wanted to throw his own words back at him and tell him he needed to have discipline, but knew better than to rub it in.

Chapter 9

Neither of them had ever been in what most people would call a relationship before. Nor had it occurred to either of them theirs was one. They were both so accustomed to transactional associations with people they failed to notice that this one was somehow different.

Zapato was quite content with their arrangement. It served his purposes well. He had succeeded where others had failed, forging a comfortable, secure second act as rancher Jean-Paul and he found he looked forward to getting out of bed each morning. As long as Mary did not overstep—and she seemed to understand the boundaries—she pleased him.

For Mary, it was increasingly a different story. As the island started opening up, she wanted to get out and go places. Jean-Paul, who had seemed to share this yearning when everything was locked down, no longer appeared to care. His interests seemed to be bound up in the ranch. He and Tommy were now talking about starting a small herd of horses, perhaps partnering with Lani in some manner. Hitting the malls, resorts, bars, and restaurants was not part of his agenda.

In more practical terms, she needed to use the car for basic purchases, because Jean-Paul forbade online ordering. It was about security. A delivery made to the ranch was a vulnerability easily avoided, he had explained. Not to mention being a pain in the ass with their gated driveway.

It came to a head over use of their only car, a Jeep. Jean-Paul was fine with Mary going out and about by herself, but he also wanted the vehicle available whenever he wanted to use it. This led to several entirely predictable conflicts. And an obvious solution.

***

Mary was reading a magazine when Jean-Paul came out on the deck. He and Tommy had gone out in Tommy's truck after lunch on some sort of errand.

"Come, I want to show you something out front," he said.

They walked through the house and out the front door together. Parked next to the Jeep was a shiny blue Lexus NX 300.

Jean-Paul gestured theatrically with his hand at the SUV, grinned and said, "What do you think?"

Mary walked completely around the car, spotted the dealer plates, and said, "It looks brand new."

"It is. And it's yours."

Retirement Plan

"Mine?"

"Yours."

Problem solved.

Mary enthusiastically showed Jean-Paul her gratitude.

* * *

A half-hour before sunset that evening, Mary pulled up in front of the most luxurious resort in Wailea. As she handed her key to the valet and told him they were there for dinner at upscale Ferraro's Ristorante, she felt a frisson of entitlement. It was a feeling so foreign to her she felt as if she had become another person.

"Yes ma'am, and welcome to the Four Season's." He gave them directions to the Italian restaurant, she put her arm through Jean-Paul's, and they headed inside. She seemed to absorb the opulence. Soon they were seated at a candlelit frontline table overlooking the pool and nearby ocean. *I belong here,* Mary thought.

After the server explained the day's specials, Jean-Paul asked her to bring them each a glass of champagne even before they perused the menu. She soon returned with the flutes and their tiny bubbles, then left the smiling couple alone.

"A toast to your new car," Jean-Paul said as he raised his glass.

"And a toast to us in our new life," Mary said as they

clinked glassed. She sipped. Took in the amazing view as the sun began to set over the ocean. And thought contentedly, *This is as good as it gets.*

As she opened her menu, she noticed Jean-Paul perusing the wine list. She bit her tongue as she almost reminded him about his alcohol restriction.

Not tonight, Mary admonished herself. It's a special occasion. I need to let him feel only good about himself.

But Jean-Paul had noticed her disapproving look. He was not pleased but chose to hide it.

* * *

Having a credit card whose bill Jean-Paul paid without question was heavenly. True, it had a low credit limit. Jean-Paul had explained that if she needed to spend more, it was probably because of a purchase that they should undertake together anyway. For Mary, who had lived either in poverty or one paycheck away from it her entire life before Jean-Paul became her benefactor, this at first seemed to be an inconsequential restriction. But it had begun to grate on her, especially as she realized it kept her from purchasing the kind of clothes and jewelry to which she felt increasingly drawn. She never asked; she didn't have to. He would say they must not draw attention to themselves. Remember their cover story. They were comfortably well off, yes, a result of his frugal life and wise investments, but not wealthy.

Retirement Plan

And now he had made an exception to that rule, and she had a brand-new, sporty luxury car that was all her own. Well, not technically hers. Jean-Paul owned it and his name was on the registration. But still.

And yet. She really hated the color, popular though it was, a bright, shiny blue. Mary thought it had no class, then wondered at that word popping into her thoughts. She could not remember ever before considering whether or not something was classy. In any case, she also disliked the car's black interior. It got hot fast and cooled down slowly.

That he had just assumed that whatever he selected would please her was annoying. More so was the thought that he had just assumed that she would be thrilled with whatever he picked out for her.

Like the credit limit, it was another form of control and a constant reminder of her dependency. Which made her feel simultaneously ungrateful and resentful. It was a new and uncomfortable emotion.

Chapter 10

Mary knew she had a daddy complex.

Her father had forced her mother to leave his protection and live in squalor when she was pregnant with her. He had been an unfeeling conman Mary had repaid by murdering two women he cared about and framing him for the second crime.

Now here she was, living with a man old enough to be her father, himself a criminal, who had never had a family of his own, let alone any acknowledged children. At least, in this case, he took good care of her.

Knowing her psychology was one thing. But the heart wants...

Mary was viscerally attracted to yet another older man. Though as far as Mary knew, this one was not a crook.

* * *

She began by suggesting at breakfast one morning that they take a trip by horseback.

Retirement Plan

"What kind of trip?" Jean-Paul asked.

"I don't know exactly. Something overnight, maybe a couple of nights. In the backcountry, you know, with a tent and all."

His plate clean, Jean-Paul finished his coffee and rose from the table. "Not my thing," he said.

A few days later, Mary found Tommy working alone on a fence. He had his shirt off and his nearly hairless, muscular torso gleamed with sweat. She handed him a bottle of water she happened to be carrying and asked where she might go on such an adventure.

"Hana would be a good ride," he said. "Two days on horseback each way. Might not see people the whole route."

"Can you help me map it?"

"Sure, but you really want to be with someone who knows the trails. They aren't exactly marked, and some of it's mighty rugged. Too easy to get lost or hurt."

"Someone like Lani?"

"Yeah. Only she's nursing that broken wrist." Lani and her horse had taken a fall a week earlier.

"Oh, right. But I'm sure I could do it by myself."

Tommy gave her a serious look. "I'm not questioning your horsemanship. But Lani's as good on a horse as you'll find and look what happened to her. You'd be all alone out there. And most of the way, there's no phone reception."

Mary put on a pout.

"And I don't want to offend, but a woman alone out there is also a worry."

"No offense. That's good advice. But it can't hurt to look at a map, can it?"

Tommy Kamaka was no fool. There was no way he would venture out on an overnight ride alone with his boss's woman. What would Jean-Paul think if he even heard that such an idiotic idea was being discussed?

Tommy liked Jean-Paul. He was what he thought of as a man's man. Strong of mind and, despite his heart condition, of body. Plain spoken and reliable. At the same time, he sensed that beneath the surface lurked a hard, dangerous man, one whose wrath Tommy did not wish to experience. He wondered how it was that this formidable person had spent decades working as a letter carrier.

Tommy understood what was really going on with Mary and knew he had to nip it in the bud before Jean-Paul got wind of it. At the same time, he did not wish to offend Mary.

* * *

Tommy came to the door and told Mary he had mapped out a trail route to Hana. When they came around the corner to the shaded side patio where he had laid out the map on a small square table, an attractive woman Mary had never seen before smiled up from her bench seat.

"This is my friend Mia," Tommy said. "She too is an able rider."

Mary extended her hand and said, "Pleased to meet you." The women lightly touched hands.

"I sure hope this works out," Mia said, as Tommy sat on the bench next to her, leaving Mary to sit catty-corner from the pair. "We could stay a couple of days in Hana and have a real backcountry trek. It'll be fun."

We? He's never mentioned a girlfriend. The two thoughts hit Mary like a one-two punch.

They discussed plans for the trip, or, more accurately, Tommy and Mia did so. Mary quickly lost interest.

That evening, as she lay in bed next to Jean-Paul, Mary fantasized about various ways of killing Mia. They all involved a handgun. It was something with which she had experience.

Chapter 11

Once a week, Rosie was permitted to clean Jean-Paul's office. Jean-Paul would unlock the door, then hang around inside the house doing something or other until Rosie finished the job.

Otherwise, the office was kept locked, in fact the door locked automatically when closed. And Mary did not have a key.

It was where Jean-Paul kept his computer, along with all his papers and records and such. He had never expressly forbidden her to enter without him present. He didn't have to. It was unambiguously understood.

Mary came to view the locked room as a symbol of Jean-Paul's power over her.

Mary was thinking about that power and her vulnerability as they left the cardiologist's Honolulu office after Jean-Paul's quarterly heart checkup. A review of lab tests had revealed no new problems since their last visit and improvements in several of Jean-Paul's numbers, which drew praise from the doctor for his positive lifestyle changes. Then they had looked at the results of his

Retirement Plan

EKG and pictures of his heart from the echocardiogram. It all looked good, the doctor said.

To Mary, it had all looked scary, seeing his insides that way. Sure, everything appeared to be fine for now, but that could change in, well, a heartbeat. Jean-Paul was not getting any younger and he had already survived two heart attacks. The third time might well be fatal. Then what would happen to her?

They had to have a serious conversation. One she knew he would not appreciate. She had to catch him at a receptive moment.

* * *

Late one afternoon, Jean-Paul was telling Mary about the horses he and Tommy had selected to start the herd. She listened raptly, asking questions to show how interested she was as he explained the issues and how each selection was made. She *was* genuinely interested, just not in the level of detail he seemed to believe necessary.

As they walked out to the barn and stable area together and Jean-Paul described his plans for yet another round of expansion, his ebullience was apparent. Mary decided it was time.

"This is all so wonderful," she began, taking his arm and leaning into his side as they strolled. "It's got me thinking. If you got sick or something, how would I take care of it all? And take care of you? I mean, I couldn't even pay the bills."

She felt him tense slightly, then slowly relax again as they continued to tour the property. He said nothing until they climbed a rise that gave them a wide vista of the ranch's acreage.

"There sure is a lot of empty land out there," Jean-Paul said.

Epilogue

Jean-Paul informed Rosie and Tommy that Mary had rushed to the airport before dawn to catch a flight to the mainland after receiving word that her elderly aunt was in desperate need of someone to care for her. Something to do with an unspecified medical emergency.

Nothing more was said of it as the days turned into weeks and Mary did not return. Rosie, who had found her mistress increasingly imperious, happily took full charge of managing the household, including planning menus to suit Jean-Paul's tastes. He even provided her with a petty cash fund that he replenished as needed. Eventually, she moved into one of the unused bedrooms.

Jean-Paul kept the Lexus. He really liked it.

Unmasked

Chapter 1

Madison Stanhope seemed to have aged rapidly since I last saw her nearly two years ago. She was still thin, tan, and blond, but the pretty, fresh-looking, California girl, who I had then pegged at about my age, 30-ish, now looked a decade older, with worry lines around her eyes and frown lines that marred the skin around her lips.

She sat down across the desk from me. We did the "I'm vaccinated, you're vaccinated, let's take off the masks" thing, then she looked around the sparsely furnished room that was the office of Brink Investigations, located over a bakery and a frozen yogurt shop in what the Campbell Chamber of Commerce earnestly touts as our quaint, historic, California downtown. "So, Joe Brink," she said, "you're a one-man operation."

"'Give me one man from among ten thousand if he is the best,'" I said.

"Is that some kind of sports thing?"

It does sound like an NFL GM on draft day. "Heraclitus, an ancient Greek philosopher."

"You're a Greek philosophy scholar?"

"No," I said, "but I had a hot philosophy professor in

college who I tried to impress with my extra credit effort."

"How'd that work out?"

"I got an A in the course."

"And the woman?"

"Struck out."

It was pleasant banter but felt forced. Now, Madison Stanhope seemed to have run out of playfulness. She forced a weak smile, sighed, rearranged herself in the chair and said, "Can we make it Maddie and Joe?"

"Sure."

"So, Joe, why am I here?"

"I'm supposed to ask you that," I said.

Maddie shook her head. "It was rhetorical. Okay, here goes. I want you to find out what happened to my husband."

She paused, as if uncertain where to go next. This felt like one of those times when the best interview technique was to keep my mouth shut. After a few beats, Maddie said, "I don't even know where to begin."

Start with a softball. "What's your husband's name?" When I'd interviewed Maddie before, he had just been "my husband."

"Steven. Steve."

"The last time I saw you, you were waiting to have a tell-all with Steve." Maddie had been a witness in a murder case I was looking into. She had found the dead body of Candice Hubbard next to her car one morning.

Unmasked

Maddie's car was parked in the lot of a San Jose apartment complex where she had spent the night with a man not her husband. The cops told her she would be a witness and they could not keep her name confidential. Maddie had told me she had decided it was better if her husband heard it from her first, and she was waiting for him to come home from a business trip to have that difficult conversation.

"Actually, that was the first time you saw me. You dropped by a couple of days later to pick up a copy of the videos from my Tesla."

My memory was duly jogged. Maddie's Tesla cameras, in sentry mode, had recorded Candice Hubbard's murder, but the car was in police custody at the time I had first seen her. After she got the car back, she let me have copies of the videos. They helped exonerate my friend Sally Rocket, who was on the verge of being arrested for Hubbard's murder.

Maddie paused again. I waited. "Anyway, Steve was already back home by the time you came for the video. Only we never had that little talk."

"Never?"

She shook her head and gave a nervous chuckle. "I chickened out. I made up a story about some problem with the car and told Steve it was in the shop. Like with so much else, he really wasn't paying attention. As long as I took care of whatever it was, that was fine by him. As time went on and I heard nothing more about my involvement in the case, saying nothing to Steve was a hell of a lot easier than the alternative. Eventually, I called Detective Taylor. He said he couldn't comment on an ongoing investigation, but I got the distinct impression the case was on the back burner. So I decided to pretend the whole thing never happened."

I nodded. I understood the scope of "whole thing." For Maddie, her indiscretion was the problem; the murder of Candice Hubbard was a side issue.

"Once my client was off the hook, I was off the case," I said. Which was true and sounded like I knew no more than Maddie did. Which was not true. The killer in that video had been identified and was still at large and wanted by the FBI, though that had not been publicized. I couldn't share any of that with Maddie even if I wanted to. It fell under the cloak of attorney-client privilege because I had been working for a lawyer on Sally's case when I learned those things. It was the sort of tap dance around the truth I often found myself doing in my work.

Maddie waved a hand in front of her face, as if shooing away gnats. "Well, it doesn't much matter anymore. Steve is dead. Murdered."

Chapter 2

Maddie filled me in on what she knew about her husband's death. I took careful notes. When she reached the end of the story, I asked her what, exactly, she wanted from me.

"I don't believe the official story. I want you to find out what really happened, who did it and why."

"You don't believe it because...?"

"They say the janitor did it. A burglary gone bad. But when they returned Steve's personal effects to me, nothing was missing, not even his watch, a Bulgari I bought for him for our tenth anniversary for about $15,000. And there was a lot of electronic equipment in that building, easy to steal and I would think easy to sell. But Chet—he's the CEO—said nothing was taken. It just doesn't feel right to me."

We discussed Maddie's legal exposure, that the spouse is always a suspect, and if we raised doubts about the version of the crime the cops had settled on, they would probably turn their attention to her. I also reminded her that they knew she had found a dead body while cheating on her now dead husband, and that was bound to set off cop alarms.

Maddie stared off into space a moment, nodded as if to herself and said, "You're right, I've been naïve. I probably should have gotten a lawyer right away. Can you refer me? The only kind of lawyers my friends seem to know are divorce lawyers."

I gave Maddie Ed Wax's phone number. I thought Ed might have a conflict of interest because he had been Sally's lawyer when she was briefly a suspect for the Candice Hubbard murder, but I figured Ed could sort that out and, at the very least, give Maddie a good referral.

"I'm going to get started on your case," I said. "Tell whoever you choose as your lawyer that you want me as part of the legal team. Assuming you do."

"Of course I do. That's why I'm here."

Before she left, I gave Maddie my client engagement agreement. From my visits to her multi-million-dollar custom home in tony Monte Sereno when I was working on the Hubbard case, I had detected that she was well off. I chose the contract with my top-tier rates. She did not bat an eyelash as she signed it and took out her checkbook.

* * *

After Maddie left, I read the news accounts of Steve

Unmasked

Stanhope's death. It had happened a month ago but had not captured my attention. From the various news articles and what Maddie had told me, along with some calls to a couple of law enforcement sources, I pieced together a narrative.

Steve Stanhope's body had been found by his admin shortly after she arrived at work in the morning. He was seated at his desk, his head on the keyboard of his laptop, and she thought he was asleep. She changed her mind when she saw the letter opener protruding from his back, and the dried blood discoloring his shirt and pooled on the carpet. The horrified woman ran back to her desk, called 9-1-1, and the wheels of official emergency response to a suspicious death were set in motion.

Stanhope, CFO at tech startup Aztound Technologies, often worked late, especially when they were closing the month, which they had been. In fact, it had also been their fiscal year end.

There was no mystery about the cause of death. The dagger-like letter opener—Maddie said it had been a gift from Aztound CEO Chet Khatri—had gone between two back ribs and penetrated Stanhope's heart from behind. Antemortem bruises on his shoulders indicated he had been held in place as he died. The manner of death was listed as homicide.

Security video showed someone entering the building after everyone aside from Steve had left for the day.

That person left a few minutes later. Next day, when the police began interviewing everyone who had access to the building, they could not locate the janitor, Javier Santiago, who turned out to be undocumented.

The news had made a big splash locally, but coverage lasted just a few days, as the San Jose Police Department had nothing more to share. Javier Santiago was their prime suspect and the search for him continued.

Maddie said she was interviewed by San Jose Homicide Detective Bart Taylor. The same detective who had handled the Hubbard case and knew all about Maddie's indiscretion.

Fortunately, Maddie had an alibi. She was visiting her ailing father in a Phoenix hospital, had arrived there the day before, spent the night with her mother, and was in the hospital the morning her husband's body was found. Her teenaged daughters had been staying with a friend because Steve could not be bothered with the childcare duties.

Maddie said she told Detective Taylor her husband had a high-pressure job, and they did not get to see each other as much as they would have liked. It was a common Silicon Valley lament. She had no idea of anyone who might want to harm Steve, knew of no enemies, nor had she any thought that he might commit suicide, however farfetched that notion was given the dagger in his back. They did not have money problems and his behavior had not been unusual of late. At no time during the interview, she told me, had she felt like a suspect.

Since that interview, Maddie's requests to Detective Taylor for additional information had been politely but firmly rebuffed. Her impression was that the investigation was over.

I knew better. Rich plus workaholic husband plus wandering wife equals suspect, regardless of alibi. Regardless of the suspected actual killer—the doer—having been identified. And for the same reason Maddie was hiring me. The killer had not taken anything, not even that obvious and enticing wristwatch. Perhaps he had not expected anyone to be there and panicked, but it at least raised the question of motive. Unless he had been hired for the hit.

I told Maddie that. Her face turned pale under her tan, and she actually gulped.

* * *

Ed Wax called late in the afternoon. As usual, he fired his sentences in a single rapid burst.

"Madison Stanhope is now my client. She knows not to talk about the case to anyone besides you and to refer the cops to me if they want to talk to her again. Nothing for me to do right now, you do your thing, let me know when you have something for me. And there's no conflict, so don't worry about it."

And that was that.

Chapter 3

Aztound Technologies was a cloud computing startup. From their website, I learned that they had something to do with hybrid cloud management, but exactly what that meant eluded me, despite the descriptions I read online. So I invited my neighbors, white-hat hackers Charles and Jonathan, over for dinner and asked them to explain hybrid cloud management. As we dug into our Chinese takeout, ever-precise Charles started my day's lesson in leading edge technology.

"A private cloud is a collection of computing resources dedicated to a specific company. Regardless of where those resources are—on your premises, in the cloud somewhere, or both—the company that uses them is responsible for managing them. On the other hand, a public cloud is a collection of computer resources shared by many customers. The service provider manages those resources."

"Like, I keep my photos on iCloud along with other Apple customers?"

Charles grinned. "Like that. And Apple runs those

servers. But you're responsible for your phone and computer."

"Okay, I sort of get that."

It was Jonathan's turn. "A hybrid cloud is a combination of public and private computer services. When a company uses a hybrid cloud, managing everything can become very complicated. That's where hybrid cloud management software comes into play. See, the public services are supposed to be managed by their providers, but the user company needs to have an overview of the whole thing. After all, if there are problems, the user company suffers the consequences."

"Sounds complicated," I said.

"It is," Jonathan said. "Which is where companies like Aztound come into play. Working with all the various kinds of cloud services, providing easy-to-use tools for a company's IT department to manage them, is a fast-growing, competitive business."

I knew Charles and Jonathan would have loved to dive into technical details of this stuff, but we were as far into the weeds as I cared to go. I asked them what they knew specifically about Aztound. It turned out, not much. As Charles summed it up, "We break into clouds, Joe. We don't manage them."

That I understood.

* * *

Unmasked

I do some of my most useful research over food. And usually could bill it to my client. It was a great perq of being a PI. So it was that, the day after my briefing from Jonathan and Charles, I set out to pick the brain of my friend Nick Marchetti, one Silicon Valley's legendary finance gurus, at Lasagna, Lasagna, a short walk from my office.

The daily special was Mama's Leftovers. The description on the menu read, "Mama decided to clean out the fridge and make lasagna out of the leftovers. Ask your server about today's creation."

We did. It turned out that Mama had leftover meatloaf, mashed potatoes and brown gravy, which she layered with the pasta. Nick and I both went for it.

After we gave our orders, Nick said, "You know we Italians have many forms of pasta, and names for all of them."

"Like the French have cheeses," I said.

"Like that. So, what do you think the ribbon pasta used in lasagna is called?"

"No idea," I said.

"It's called lasagna, Joe," Nick said with a gotcha chuckle. "As far back as the Middle Ages, Mama's Leftovers was no joke, it was a way to make a casserole out of whatever was available. What we think of as traditional lasagna is an Americanized thing, like chow mein."

Who needs fortune cookies when you can get pearls

of wisdom from Nick Marchetti?

"Well, I guess it's time for me to earn my dinner," Nick said.

I raised my glass of the Bardolino Nick had selected. "You always do."

We clinked glasses, sipped, and Nick began. "Aztound Technologies was formed a few years ago by Chet Khatri, backed by Greg Culpepper and Garrett Manfort, two of the top VCs in the Valley. I hear they plan to announce an IPO soon. They seem to have a good product and sound management. They've managed to gain traction and become a top-tier player in a crowded market."

Our empty salad plates were replaced by the lasagna. Mama had done herself proud, and we sat quietly enjoying our meal. When the waiter came by to refill our wineglasses, I said, "What do you know about Steve Stanhope?"

"A real shame, him dying like that. I never met him, but I asked around and heard good things. He'd been involved in a couple of startups backed by the Aztound VCs. They both ended up being acquired. In the process the VCs learned to trust him. They tend to like their startup CFOs to be conservative and forthcoming. Which seems to have described Steve Stanhope. Anyway, Aztound would have been his first IPO."

"Did you pick up anything about his murder?"

Unmasked

"Nothing that hasn't been in the news. But it's curious how quickly that dried up."

That it was. Something else to investigate. Which is what I do. It says so on my business card and on my office door. Brink Investigations.

Chapter 4

The morning after my dinner with Nick, with my big insurance fraud case all tidied up, I began my investigation into Steve Stanhope's death in earnest.

After my usual morning run and second breakfast, I called Steve's work number, which I had gotten from Maddie. I really wanted to talk to his admin, Amanda Aparicio, but Maddie didn't have her direct number; she said she had never needed it, she had always called Steve direct on his cell phone.

"Aztound Technologies. How can I help you?"

"Steve Stanhope, please."

"I'm sorry, sir. Mr. Stanhope is no longer with us. May I direct your call elsewhere?"

I'll say he's no longer with you. "May I speak to his admin, please?" *You know, the one who discovered his body.*

"I'm sorry, sir. Ms. Aparicio is also no longer with us."

That was a surprise. I politely ended the call, then did a quick online search for Amanda Aparicio. There

Unmasked

was just one hit in Santa Clara County, a 42-year-old, single woman who resided in Sunnyvale.

I had lied to Maddie. Well, not exactly lied, just misled her for the sake of a great quip. I was no longer a one-man operation. I now had an assistant, Ricky Clancy, working toward his PI license under my supervision. Given my cramped quarters, Ricky mostly worked from home and his car.

I called and asked Ricky to take a drive by the Sunnyvale address to get the lay of the land. About an hour later he called me.

"You want to see this woman?"

"That I do," I said. Until proven otherwise I would assume she was the one I was looking for.

"Then you better hustle. There are guys here packing up the house, like for moving."

"Is she there?"

"I think so. The window coverings are gone, and I can see a woman in the living room giving directions to the movers. And there's a sweet car in the driveway."

I told Ricky to stay put and headed out.

* * *

Amanda Aparicio lived on a cul-de-sac in a tract of 1950s-era ranch-style houses on small lots, much like the home I grew up in and where my parents still lived.

It looked like a neighborhood transitioning up the middle-class ladder, as skyrocketing home prices encouraged those with plenty of equity to cash out and often flee the high cost of living in Silicon Valley, heading to a lower cost of living locale. It was not unusual for the buyer to pay over a million dollars and then tear the old house down and build a McMansion. As I drove through the tract, I spotted a couple of such teardowns and several more major remodels underway.

I spotted Ricky parked across the street from the house. Somehow, he made it look like he and his nondescript car belonged there. No need for the neighbors to become concerned.

I parked on the street behind an unmarked white van. The house looked original—no additions, no second story, still with a carport instead of a garage. But it appeared well-maintained, as did the modest landscaping. And there was a new-looking Audi SUV in the carport.

The front door was wide open. Wearing a mask, I rang the bell. Amanda Aparicio greeted me. She looked a lot like Madison Stanhope, trim, tan and fit, but where Maddie was blond and blue-eyed, Amanda was raven-haired, with rich brown eyes. Like those doll brands, where they have pretty much the same doll with different hair, eye, and skin colors.

I introduced myself and handed her my card. Told her I was working for Mrs. Stanhope and asked if I

Unmasked

could speak to her for a few minutes. She appeared taken aback, a response I often get, but in what appeared to be an almost reflexive act of politeness, invited me inside. She did not ask who in the world Mrs. Stanhope was; clearly, this was the Amanda Aparicio I sought.

The good manners continued as she offered me a cold can of Diet Pepsi, apologetically saying that the fridge was otherwise empty, so it was that or water. I believe Diet Pepsi is what we'll be forced to drink if we run out of Diet Coke, but I chose not to mention it.

After she got the cans from the kitchen, we sat down in the living room on folding chairs at a card table, surrounded by moving boxes of various sizes. I unmasked and sipped the ersatz cola. The furniture was wrapped in heavy-duty plastic, carpets had been rolled up and tied, and there was a stack of padded blankets in the middle of the room. From time to time, a guy would appear from elsewhere in the house, head out to the van, and return with empty cartons or packing material.

I noticed a couple of suitcases in the corner, a heavy winter jacket draped over the extended handle of one of them.

I sought to establish rapport. "It looks like you're moving," I said.

"You really are a detective, aren't you, Mr. Brink?"

"None better. And please call me Joe."

"I'm Amanda. You said you were working for Maddie?"

"Yes. She wants to find out more about what happened to her husband."

Amanda nodded. "They say that the janitor killed him."

"Actually, he's a suspect. The case is still open."

She shrugged. "I don't know anything more than what I already told the police." Then she shook her head. "Finding him like that…"

We both sipped our sodas. It was Amanda's turn to stare off into space a few moments. I was struck again by how much she looked like Maddie. Then she regrouped and said, "Here's the thing. I can't talk to you about anything related to the company or my work for Steve. I can't talk to anyone except the police about his death or anything I know about him. I signed an NDA to that effect. I like Maddie, we used to share a giggle about the confusion, and I'd like to help her get the answers she needs, but my hands are tied. I'm sorry if you wasted your time coming here."

Foiled again by the pervasive Silicon Valley non-disclosure agreement. I grasped at a straw to keep her talking. "The confusion?"

"You know, our names. Maddie, Mandy. Caused all sorts of funny mix-ups."

Ah, yes. Amanda. Mandy. Maddie. Cute. Time for one more try.

Unmasked

"About that NDA. Do you know what would happen if you were subpoenaed by Mrs. Stanhope's lawyer?" I thought that might intimidate her into cooperating. Or it could end our budding rapport. Amanda surprised me.

"My instructions are to refer any such thing to Aztound's attorney," she said coolly. "Look, it's not that I want to keep any secrets. I'm not even sure I know any that matter. It's just that my settlement means a lot to me, and I won't do anything to jeopardize it."

"Settlement?"

"I just can't work there anymore. Too many bad images in my head, I get a panic attack just thinking about being there. The company understood and gave me a generous severance package. Now I'm moving near Melanie in Austin." She waved a hand expansively. "The mover is picking up all this stuff this afternoon, then I'm flying off to my new life. So, please give Maddie my best, but I'm afraid I just can't help you." She rose and motioned to escort me to the front door. I had apparently exhausted my quota of polite.

I shrugged and handed Amanda my card. "If you change your mind or think of anything you're willing to tell me that would help Maddie, please contact me. And enjoy your flight to Austin."

She took the card and walked me to the door.

I got in my car and called Ricky, who was still loitering across the street. My instructions were brief.

Phil Bookman

I was cruising down 85, heading back to Campbell, when I got a text from Ed Wax. **Meet Stanhope my office 4:00 today.** I replied thumbs up. There was no sense wondering what this was about; I'd find out in a few hours.

* * *

Later, after UPS and the moving van had come and gone, Amanda locked the front door behind her and wheeled her suitcases out to her new car.

That cop, Detective Taylor, who looked like he had seen it all and then some, had made her nervous, but she had been prepared and felt she had handled herself well. Joe Brink, on the other hand, seemed like a pushover. He was so young and...earnest, that was the word. Still wet behind the ears. Even though he had surprised her, showing up unannounced, she had managed just fine. She couldn't help herself, she had toyed with him, given him a bit of a runaround, just for the fun it. Along with sowing a few seeds of deception.

Amanda tossed the ski jacket onto the front passenger seat of the SUV, then loaded the luggage in the back. *I won't miss this goddamn house or any of that old crap.* The house had become an albatross after Juan died. Huge mortgage and property tax payments, expensive utilities, and constant repairs. Add to that their foolish choice of a costly out-of-state school for

Melanie. Bottom line was that Amanda had constantly struggled to support herself and the kids. She had already been working as an admin for a few years before Juan's accident, but it had taken both their incomes to keep up with the cost of living in Silicon Valley.

She had briefly considered selling the house and moving to a cheaper part of the country; she'd be able to get out from under and use the equity to help the kids with college and get herself resettled. But her son had been struggling after his father's passing, in all the ways only a teenage boy could. His situation had been precarious; the disruption of a move was a bad idea. Thankfully, her daughter, as always, was doing great and her son had finally gotten back on track.

I've worked my ass off for years to make ends meet and take care of my kids. Now it's my turn.

Amanda started the Audi, backed out of the driveway, and drove away.

Chapter 6

Back in the office, I decided to spend some time researching Amanda Aparicio and her family. I had been about to do that earlier when Ricky's call made me scurry out unprepared.

Since I had opened my own PI business, I had of necessity gotten pretty good at online investigation. I was not only proficient with various search engines, including some specialized ones, I had also learned from Charles and Jonathan how to discreetly—meaning untraceably—hack into certain databases I should not have been able to access.

By mid-afternoon, I had put together a pretty good profile. Born Amanda Estrada in 1978 in San Jose, Amanda married Juan Aparicio, who worked as a butcher in an upscale market, in 1996 when she was 19. She gave birth to a daughter that same year, and a son two years later.

Daughter Melanie, now 24, graduated from the University of Texas and worked for a tech company in Austin. Son Raymond, 22, was a senior at Fresno State, where he had transferred after two years at Mission College.

Amanda appeared to have been a stay-at-home mom until she went to work when her kids were in high school as an admin at the company Steve Stanhope was with before Aztound Technologies. It looked like he brought her with him to Aztound.

Juan Aparicio had died in an auto accident four years ago, leaving his wife with a daughter paying whopping out-of-state tuition at the University of Texas, a son heading for college, and a newly refinanced mortgage with a $3,000 monthly payment. I wondered if the college choices for Raymond had been made for financial reasons.

The Aparicio's had purchased the Sunnyvale home in 2006, at the height of the real-estate bubble, for $700,000, with very little down and two variable-rate mortgages. Like many, they had weathered the crash, which saw property values plummet and interest on those mortgages reset much higher than they had expected. My guess was that they had been underwater for a few years before they were able to refinance. Then property values soared yet again as Silicon Valley went into another boom cycle. Amanda's house was now worth about a million dollars.

I got the $1,000,000 figure from a real estate website that provided neighborhood comps. It also revealed that her property was in the market's sweet spot, just below the average Silicon Valley price.

County records showed Amanda had sold her house for $995,000 just days ago. I deduced that was why there had been a SOLD sign out front. A call to a realtor friend confirmed that the sales price was just about right for that neighborhood, and, in the current market, would have sold quickly.

I checked housing prices in Austin. The median home price was about $400,000 versus over $1,000,000 in Silicon Valley. I could understand the appeal.

As I left for the drive to Ed Wax's office near the courthouse in downtown San Jose, I considered what I had learned. I had more questions than answers.

Amanda had certainly relocated quickly. Was that to get far away from prying investigators, be they police, press or private? She had made a tidy profit from the sale of the house. I wondered what the severance package she had mentioned entailed.

If she was flying to Austin, why did she have a ski jacket with her luggage? According to my weather app, temperatures in Austin this week were in the 80s, and it had been near that all week here. And what was she going to do with her brand-new SUV? Leave it at the airport in long-term parking where the temporary tags would act like a homing beacon for car thieves?

* * *

Unmasked

Just before it was time for me to leave for the meeting at Ed Wax's office, Ricky called.

"A truck picked up her stuff. Like, two trucks. First, UPS took some real large cartons. Then came a big truck from East Valley Furniture Warehouse, you know, the used furniture place that buys your stuff and resells it? They got ads all over TV? It looked to me like they probably emptied the place. Anyway, a few minutes later, the Audi pulled out. It was an easy tail; traffic was light, and she seemed oblivious. Drove out 280, up 680, then got onto 80 east. We just passed Sacramento. You want me to keep following?"

That was over two hours away. I called Ricky off and thanked him.

"One more thing, Joe. Did you notice those temporary plates were from Colorado?"

And I'm the licensed PI? "Good catch, I missed that. Before you break off, see if you can spot the name of the dealer."

"Will do."

A few moments later, Ricky called again, "The license plate holder says Glenwood Springs Audi, wherever that is."

"Thanks, Ricky."

Google told me Glenwood Springs Audi was in the town of Glenwood Springs, Colorado, in the Rocky Mountains about 150 miles due west of Denver.

Amanda was not moving her furniture to Austin. Nor had she been heading to any of the Bay Area airports to fly there. But she was driving in the right direction for Colorado.

My hunch was she had sent her clothes and whatnot via UPS. Maybe shipped the kids their stuff that they still had at home as well. And sold the rest to East Valley Furniture Warehouse.

I was used to being lied to for all sorts of reasons. But why, I wondered, had Amanda Aparicio, who was under no obligation to even talk to me, bothered to concoct such a flaky story? And why that particular fairy tale?

Chapter 7

They needed to hire a new CFO. Like yesterday.

Greg Culpepper sat in his Sand Hill Road office at Culpepper Capital Management and stared at his phone, as if the solution to his problem would somehow magically appear on its screen. He had just ended a call with a worried Chet Khatri. Howard Penning, Aztound's controller, was competent enough to fill in for his deceased boss for a while—he could keep the trains running on time, manage to complete the year-end closing—but he was no CFO. If they were going to file for an IPO, they had to hire a new chief financial officer who could not only handle the IPO process but would give investors and analysts confidence.

Time to stop staring at the phone and use it. Distasteful though it was, Culpepper knew he had to call Manfort.

* * *

Greg Culpepper and Garrett Manfort, head of Manfort

Venture Partners, had teamed up with Chet Khatri to form Aztound Technologies six years ago. Khatri had one successful startup under his belt, his pitch was good, and both VCs had wanted a hybrid cloud management company to fill a hole in their portfolios.

They had brought Steve Stanhope in as CFO. Manfort had worked with Stanhope before and touted his sound judgement and business skills. Whatever he thought of Manfort personally, Culpepper respected the man's judgement when it came to key personnel. Culpepper had spent some time with Stanhope, as had Khatri, and they agreed he was the right man for the job. Though he had grown up in L.A. and gotten his MBA from USC, Stanhope had the kind of earnest, honest, almost-but-not-quite handsome face and middle American politeness that exuded integrity. At the same time, his finance and general business knowledge were excellent. Sound and focused were the words both men used to describe Steve Stanhope.

Everything had gone well, Culpepper mused, until Stanhope was murdered at his desk. *Murdered!* By a Mexican janitor who had then taken off, probably back across the border by now. Culpepper was happy to leave that to the police. His most pressing problem, Aztound's problem, was that he, Khatri and Manfort could not agree on a new CFO.

As much as possible, Culpepper avoided talking to Garrett Manfort. The man was a mean, unpleasant son

Unmasked

of a bitch. Problem was, he had the Midas touch when it came to making money. And in Greg Culpepper's world, making boatloads of money trumped pretty much everything else. If he had to deal with a miserable prick like Garrett Manfort, so be it.

But he did not have to like it.

Culpepper placed the call.

* * *

Garrett Manfort roared into the phone like an irate lion. "What now?"

Greg Culpepper winced at Manfort's dismissive rudeness. Culpepper, Manfort's peer in the upper echelon of the Silicon Valley VC pecking order, was used to at least respect and often deference from movers and shakers around the world. But not from this narcissistic bully. Yet Culpepper always hoped...for what? He felt like Charlie Brown, foolishly expecting that Lucy would not move the football this time.

Culpepper had long ago learned that Manfort was impervious to retorts, be they sarcastic, ironic, angry, whatever. Best to just get to the point.

"I just got off the phone with Chet. We need to make a CFO decision now or we could miss the IPO window."

"My guy is ready to start," Manfort said impatiently. "Just say the word."

"He doesn't have IPO experience," Culpepper said.

"Deepa Patel does. It's that simple."

"Neither did Stanhope. And I say that little gal you and Chet have such a crush on doesn't have the balls for the job."

And you're a goddamn misogynist. "We outvote you," Culpepper said calmly. Each of the VC firms had two board seats. CEO Chet Khatri had the fifth. And Culpepper was board chair because Khatri abstained, and he had won the coin toss. "I'm going to tell Chet to make the offer."

"You can't do that," Manfort bellowed.

"Yes," Culpepper said calmly, "we can."

Manfort let loose a string of expletives. Smiling, Greg Culpepper ended the call leaving the asshole in mid-rant.

Chapter 8

Stepping into Ed Wax's office on North First Street was like going back in time about a century. Real wood paneling, brass fixtures, hardwood floors and crown moldings were complemented by oak rolltop desks, tables, file cabinets and chairs, and antique-looking lamps.

Ed, too, was a throwback. In an era of legal specialization, he was a generalist, doing, as he often said, whatever legal work his clients required, aided by two associates, a paralegal, and a secretary. But he knew his limits; Ed Wax had a wide network of legal specialists to call upon when "whatever legal work his clients required" warranted it.

He also had an as-needed investigator. Me.

Maddie Stanhope and I arrived within a few minutes of each other and were immediately shown into Ed's office. The three of us sat around a small oak conference table in matching wooden chairs and Ed, as was his habit, skipped the preliminaries. Locking his eyes with mine, he said, "The situation's changed. For some reason, Taylor wanted to re-interview Maddie. She told him to contact me. Good girl. We met with Taylor and his partner here this morning. Pissed them off that I refused to meet on their turf. Too bad.

"They wouldn't answer any of my questions, like what about this Santiago? So, either they think our client was in cahoots with him or they're exploring other theories of the crime.

"Anyway, we didn't give them anything they didn't already know, but now that we know what they have, or think they have, it's time for us to find out everything we can from our client."

"What do they have?"

"Two things," Ed said, still talking to me as if Maddie weren't there. "The usual biggies. The state of the marriage and money. But no hard evidence."

"Because there is none," Maddie said, asserting her presence. "Sure, my marriage wasn't the greatest, but I had nothing to do with Steve's murder. And I never heard of that janitor."

We all knew that Detective Taylor was already aware of discord in the Stanhope marriage. He had been the detective on the Candice Hubbard homicide, when Maddie had asked him to keep her indiscretion—spending the night with a guy she picked up in a bar while her husband was out of town on business—under wraps. I had never questioned Maddie about the extent of the marital problems. It was time for that now, and Maddie knew it, because, when I prompted her, she

Unmasked

started right in.

"I feel so damn unoriginal. Steve was at work a lot—I mean, he even went in during the lockdown—and even when he was with us, he wasn't really with us. He was always on a call or reading email or spreadsheets, thinking about his business. Sounds like a Silicon Valley cliché, right? Anyway, this had been going on for years. I took care of the kids and the house and even managed our money." She grimaced and shook her head. "He was a CFO, but he could hardly be bothered with family finances. Meanwhile, I bitched to my friends. And every once in a while, I went out for a little adult play. Like that night that poor woman got murdered."

"I'm sure the cops talked to some of those friends recently," I said.

"I know they did, I heard from a couple of them."

"Was he unfaithful or abusive?"

"Abusive, no. Unfaithful? I thought maybe but I was never sure. If he was, he was careful. I never saw any unusual checks or anything suspicious on our credit card statements, but Steve had a company card and I never saw those charges. He travelled sometimes on business and who knows what he did then. When I think back on it, I realize how separate our lives were for a long time. It used to make me angry. Now, it just makes me sad."

I could tell that Ed was getting antsy, uninterested

in how Maddie felt about things. He was a just-the-facts guy. I had learned to be patient, to let a subject tell their story their own way.

I then went through the standard litany of PI questions in a case like this, some of which I had asked when I last saw Maddie, but now, with the stakes higher, they were worth repeating. And Ed would also be hearing her answers this time. Did she know anyone who had a grudge against Steve? Any threats? Any unusual activity or change of behavior or spending? Maddie said the police had asked all of those things early on, multiple times, but she really had nothing to offer. Steve's life outside the home was opaque to her, their conversations limited to the mundane minutiae of everyday life, and not even much of that.

Steve, she said, knew a lot of people but she couldn't think of anyone she though he would have called a close personal friend. Mostly business acquaintances. Some with strong personalities, some he had conflicts with, but nothing he had told her about that stood out. And none they socialized with.

"What about Amanda Aparicio?"

"His admin? They sure spent enough time together, but I never suspected anything between them. I mean, she's my age, maybe older. I always imagined Steve with some young bimbo. I'll say this, he sure didn't have much energy left for me, but I always blamed it on work and stress. Maybe I was fooling myself. Anyway,

Unmasked

I hardly knew anyone at the company, Amanda included."

"Was he having trouble at work?"

"That was Steve's world, not mine. We used to talk about our days, but over the years he had become more and more closemouthed about work. Which, being all he appeared interested in, did not leave us much to talk about. Which seemed fine with him."

"Let's talk about the money," Ed said. We did.

Maddie had been the family money manager and they had sound investments, all of which were now hers. More, Steve's death had produced a gigantic payout for his wife. He had life insurance tied to the mortgage, so Maddie was about to own a house worth at least $4 million free and clear. Steve had other life insurance that totaled over $7 million. His Aztound stock could be worth millions, depending on the IPO, and the company had offered to pay her his salary for the rest of the year, including a year-end bonus, on the condition that Maddie sign a non-disclosure agreement.

"I had procrastinated with that legal paperwork. Then Ed advised me not to sign, so I didn't. Now the bastards took the deal off the table.

"Anyway, the life insurance was all with the same company. Also bastards. They had been dragging their feet with me, but one call from Ed and, like magic, they found the paperwork and wired the funds. What a relief!"

Ed, unimpressed by this small triumph and uninterested in what he already knew, waved his hand in a "move it along" gesture.

"Today, Detective Taylor said he knew about the insurance," Maddie said. "He flat out stated that Steve's death had made me rich and gotten me out of an unhappy marriage. That's when Ed said the interview was over and told him to leave."

Ed's body language told me he was once more losing interest. He said to Maddie, "I want Joe to get hard evidence that makes your alibi airtight. Then if the cops still stay focused on you, it'll be because they think you hired Santiago to do the job. So, your exposure is that they somehow get what they think is evidence of that and arrest you. At this point, we want to be sure that doesn't happen. Which gets us back to why you hired us in the first place. We need to find out what really happened. Which is also what Joe does."

Chapter 9

The great thing about cell phones is that the phone goes where the person goes. You don't have to wonder if they're home or at their office the way adults always did when I was a kid. Sure, you had to know the phone number, but, hey, I'm a trained professional investigator.

Wherever Melanie Aparicio was, she answered my call. "Ms. Aparicio, my name is Joe Brink. I'm a detective working on the case involving your mother's boss, Steve Stanhope." There was no need to mention that I'm a *private* detective.

"Omigod, that was so awful. Is my mom okay?"

"As far as I know, Mandy is fine."

"Mandy? Oh, you mean Amanda."

"Right. I was just talking to her earlier today, then she left to head your way."

"My way? You must have misunderstood. Mom's not coming to Austin."

"Let me check my notes." I did. "That's what I wrote down. 'Flying to Austin to be near Melanie.'"

A giggle flooded my ear. "Mom's moving to Aspen, silly, not Austin. To a condo near Melanie Griffith's mansion, not me. Only I think she sold it a while ago. Melanie Griffith, I mean. But Mom says they still call it, like, Melanie's Mansion. Anyway, can you believe Mom's new place comes furnished? And she has an indoor pool and spa? So cool. I'm pretty sure she's not flying; she's driving there over the next few days."

It took me a moment to sort out that tossed word salad. "Oh, yeah, I must have heard her wrong," I said, wondering what else I could have gotten wrong.

As if not hearing me, Melanie gushed on. "And my school loans and credit cards? Mom just paid them off for me! Raymond's too! Now my credit score will go up. Like, I'm free at last."

I doubt that was what Martin Luther King had in mind. I chatted with Melanie a little more. The only other useful thing she gave me was that her mother had a new job involving something at a ski lodge, though the name of the employer and nature of the work escaped her. Although she seemed unfiltered and forthcoming in the extreme, she knew nothing else relevant, let alone how to express it clearly. I was willing to deal with the latter to get something that might be useful, one of a PI's many burdens.

Call ended, I wondered if Melanie wondered exactly why I had called her; I had never said. Then I thought back to my interview with Amanda. She might have

Unmasked

said she was going to be near Melanie in Aspen, and I had just heard it as Austin, but I didn't think so. At that point, I hadn't yet done my research and had no idea her daughter was in Austin; the city wasn't in my awareness yet. I had intentionally repeated it, wishing her a good flight to Austin, in an effort to engage her a bit longer. She had not corrected me about the mode of transportation or the destination. Then again, some people say, "I have to fly" when they mean "go." And Aspen would explain the ski jacket, the new Audi 4x4 SUV, and the drive east on I-80.

A quick search confirmed that the actress Melanie Griffith had indeed sold her huge Aspen cabin in 2019. Then Google Maps gave me another clue: Glenwood Springs was 40 miles northeast of Aspen. Hmmm.

Had Amanda Aparicio deliberately misled me? If so, it was a ruse that would hardly stand up to the most casual investigation. So, why bother?

And what was the deal with the nickname Mandy that her daughter, airhead though she might be, had balked at?

Regardless, it was clear that Steve Stanhope's death had worked out quite well financially for Amanda Aparicio and her children.

* * *

Maddie Stanhope's alibi held up.

In addition to her mother backing her story, I had airline records verifying that she was on the flights she had claimed to have taken to and from Phoenix. I had two nurses who remembered her being at the hospital with her father, whom they verified was a very sick man. One said she had been there until late the night Steve had been killed, the other, that she had returned early the following morning. I had phone records of calls and texts to her kids, though none to her husband, during that period, and geolocation confirmation that her phone had been where she said she was.

I fired off an email summarizing all that to Ed Wax.

Maddie could not have killed her husband.

Chapter 10

Roxie Roxbury, Aztound Technologies' one and only accounts payable clerk, listened to the cacophony of raised voices and other random sounds of office frenzy, sipped her coffee, and smiled. Her cube was an island of sanity amidst the tempestuous chaos of fiscal year-end in the accounting department.

Roxie thought of these periodic storms like the hurricanes she had experienced as a child growing up in South Carolina. Month-end was a category 1: expect minor damage, and it happened so often that you had to be prepared for it as a routine annoyance. Quarter-end was a category 2: extensive damage, batten down the hatches, stock up on food, water, batteries, and toilet paper, and prepare to ride it out. Year-end was a category 3 or higher: devastation was coming, prepare to evacuate.

The problem was that evacuation was not an option. There were no acceptable excuses for accounting staff to be off work during year-end closing. And now, that meant physically present in the office. Which often led to casualties.

This time, they had the added chaos of closing the books without a chief financial officer. Poor Howie, the controller, was going nuts, hounded by the CEO, board members and their outside auditor.

Though occasionally she stayed late to show solidarity with her peers, in truth these periodic tempests never touched Roxie's bill-paying haven. She chuckled to herself as she considered the plant in its pot atop her file cabinet. *Bill-paying isn't exactly right. More like bill-payment-delaying.*

Like those hurricanes, each vendor was categorized. Category 1: payment would be made 30 days from the time the invoice was approved for payment by the responsible manager, regardless of when the invoice was received. Category 2: 60 days. Category 3: 90 days, and then only after the vendor called asking for the money. There were a few exceptions to this scheme, each with a specific payment schedule, like taxes and utilities, but not many.

Most vendors were category 2. That was the default the computer assigned. Only the CEO or CFO could authorize category 1. Category 3 was referred to in the accounting department as the doghouse. It was where a vendor was sent when no one who mattered gave a shit about doing future business with them.

Some fools in category 2 called and berated Roxie, demanding their money. They must not have realized that she could relegate a vendor to the doghouse with a few mouse clicks. *People should know you never want to piss off an AP clerk,* Roxie silently told her potted plant.

She liked that plant. It was some kind of succulent with fat leaves. It could go ages without water or any other attention. Like her, it seemed to thrive on being left alone. But what she liked the best was that it listened attentively to her and never talked back. She had another just like it at home, the only living thing besides herself in her condo.

Roxie easily handled AP all by herself. Most of it was automated. Vendors set up their accounts and submitted invoices online. Items received on the loading dock and in the mailroom were entered into the system there. Managers were notified automatically if an invoice needed their approval, and they did so online. Payments were made electronically. And so on. Roxie's work consisted mainly of administering the AP portion of the system and dealing with questions, problems, and exceptions.

The reason the periodic accounting maelstroms never touched Roxie was that there was no last-minute scrambling in accounts payable to get things tidied up for closing the books. Who cared if a bill was paid before the close? Short-term obligations—bills still owed—were debited, subtracted, from cash-on-hand on the closing reports. Pay a bill, you reduced cash but also reduced the AP debit. Don't pay it and you increased cash but also increased the debit. It produced the same result either way.

Sure, the company might have a cash crunch, in which case she would just delay more payments. But Aztound was well-funded and had a healthy credit line. Cash management was not an issue.

No, let the poor chumps in accounts receivable, payroll, general ledger and contracting go nuts getting their ducks lined up for the drama of the big close. The peace and quiet and obscurity of accounts payable suited Roxie Roxbury just fine.

I think I'll give you a little water today, she told her plant.

Chapter 11

Detective Bart Taylor walked into my office, carefully placed a small white bag in the center of my desk, peeled off his mask and plopped down into a chair across from me.

"Only reason I'm here is to say hello to Sally." He said, referring to Sally Rocket, owner and operator of the recently reopened Sally Rocket Studio across the hall.

"And yet you brought what looks suspiciously like a bag of donuts."

"Once more, the young PI shows promise. Yes, the bag contains donuts from the bakery downstairs."

"Whose donuts you have previously designated world-class," I said.

"I, being a cop, have the power vested in me to bestow that designation. But I must periodically perform quality testing, lest they slip."

"Lest?"

Bart's normal scowl intensified. "You would mock a brother for saying lest?"

"'Get me some poison, Iago, this night. I'll not expostulate with her, lest her body and beauty unprovide my mind again,'" I said.

Bart flashed a *what the hell?* look.

"Othello," I said. "Shakespeare's Moor. Another black man saying lest."

"I know who Othello was," he said. "But how do you know those lines?"

"I had a girlfriend in college who majored in theater arts and got me to take a class which mainly involved putting on that play. She got the role of Desdemona. I understudied for Iago. She dumped me for the guy who played Roderigo."

"Some memory," Bart said. "For those lines, I mean. They weren't even yours."

"My eidetic memory is both a blessing and a curse," I said solemnly. I don't have one; eidetic was one of my vocabulary builder app's bonus words that month.

Bart shook his head in mock sadness. "Eidetic? Can we stop this shit?"

"I'm just getting warmed up," I said.

"Maybe I should take my donuts and go." He reached for the bag.

I snatched it away. In a pinch, my reflexes were excellent. "Okay," I said, "I'll behave." I reached into the bag and extracted an apple crumb. I handed the bag back to Bart, who fished out a glazed. Silently congratulating myself for getting first dibs, I went over to my

Unmasked

little fridge and got us both sodas. I grabbed some paper towels off the table next to the fridge to use as napkins.

I had remained maskless when Bart arrived, so was already prepared to sample his selections. We silently enjoyed our donuts. I finished mine and took another, a jelly this time, and said, "Since you were only here visiting Sally, you did not stop in to tell me you can't tell me anything about the Stanhope case." It wasn't a question.

"Nice double negative. You remember the last time Maddie Stanhope was involved in a case?"

"I do."

"You remember we saw the killer do it on video but couldn't find them?"

And you at first thought it was Sally. "You know I do."

"Anyway, the brass loves it when we solve a case fast but hates the 'couldn't find them' part. I too hate it when that happens."

"And now, it's happening again," I said, shaking my head, doing my best to look and sound sympathetic.

Bart actually rolled his eyes, then popped the last bit of his donut into his mouth, chewed and swallowed contentedly, and said, "I can't talk about the Stanhope case."

"But after looking for your suspect for a month or so," I said, "maybe you've been told to try harder."

Again, not a question.

"You have a talent for understatement. And maybe sometimes there's pressure to close a case fast, then someone higher up the chain has a different idea. You know what they say about shit rolling downhill. Guess who's at the bottom of this stinking hill?"

Bart selected another donut and became absorbed in it. I decided to take a flyer. "I sure wish I could see the autopsy report. Assuming the newsies got it right, it would have taken considerable strength or skill to plunge that letter opener between the back ribs and then hold him down while he bled out. Maybe getting it between the ribs was lucky. Maybe hitting the heart was too. I also wonder about the angle of entry, what the tox screen turned up, any other goodies the autopsy might reveal. And it would be great to know the ME's window for time of death."

I took a bite of my jelly donut. It dripped. I wiped. The red jelly made me think of Steve Stanhope's blood oozing from the wound in his back. "I'm not going to see the autopsy report, am I?"

Bart wiped his fingers, dabbed his lips, lowered his voice an octave, and solemnly intoned, "Autopsy reports are medical records. Unless presented as evidence in a trial, they are subject to HIPAA privacy rules." He took a bite of donut. His voice returned to normal. "But, if you were stabbed in the heart, it typically wouldn't take much strength to hold you down.

Unmasked

Just saying."

He took his notebook and a pen out of his pocket, found the page he was looking for, and wrote something on the used paper towel in front of him. Then he grabbed the donut bag and left. It was not yet empty.

* * *

The last time Bart had slipped me a love note like that, it had been the address of someone I'd been searching for. Just like then, we were alone in my office, the door was closed, so why not just tell me instead of slipping me the love note? I figured it was because he remembered the time someone had bugged my office. Or maybe he just liked a bit of cloak and dagger. Regardless, this time he had left me two strings of numbers to decipher.

The first started with 91 followed by a space. Google told me it was the country code for India. I called the number. Though it was the middle of the night there, I reached a live person at Honorable Swordworks which, I was told, had been manufacturing swords and daggers since the time of the British Raj. Today, they made replicas of the weapons they once supplied to the colonial British Army, for collectors, props in reenactments, plays and movies. In response to my query, the helpful woman with the pleasant, lilting accent said, yes, the daggers were also marketed as letter openers,

Phil Bookman

sold in India at souvenir shops. Or I could order online.

I thanked her, then went to the website and entered the second string of digits Bart had left me in the search box. Good guess. It was the SKU for a dagger-cum-letter-opener. The page was complete with a picture and detailed description. It had a steel blade, gold-plated guard, black rubber-coated hilt and gold-plated pommel. I got those names from a labelled image a Google search for "sword parts" supplied. No dimensions or weight were listed.

I was two for two. Made me feel like such a competent detective.

The implement in the photo had a pointy tip. I wondered how sharp the blade was. I called back my new friend, who revealed that all the daggers were intentionally dull, about the sharpness of a butter knife. "They are replicas, sir, not the real thing. We don't want anyone to cut themselves!" However, she assured me, the point was quite pointy. Fine for opening letters.

"Are they sturdy. I mean, if I stabbed something like a slab of, um, lamb, would it break?" I caught myself just in time; I had almost said beef before I remembered those videos of cows roaming in the streets and markets of India. Sacred cows. I wondered if that was where we got "holy cow" from. Then I refocused.

"They are most certainly sturdy, sir. The finest quality for 150 years. But not intended for use in food preparation or as cutlery."

Unmasked

I didn't think Honorable Swordworks had been making letter opener replica daggers 150 years ago but kept that to myself.

I ordered one for $99 plus expedited shipping, which I would bill to Ed Wax, who I knew would add it to his invoice to Maddie Stanhope.

Chapter 12

As Garrett Manfort drove home from his Sand Hill Road office to his Atherton estate, he pondered the Aztound Technologies situation.

Manfort made it a habit to have someone loyal to him on the executive team of each company he invested in. At Aztound Technologies, that had been Steve Stanhope.

He had spotted Stanhope's potential years ago, when the young man was one of the faceless soldiers in the army of interchangeable grunts employed by a major accounting firm. Stanhope had been working on the audit team for a company Manfort had backed. He saw that Stanhope was risk-averse but ambitious. Ultimately, the two struck a deal. Manfort would see to it that Stanhope always had a job as CFO of one of Manfort's portfolio companies. In return, Stanhope would be Manfort's inside eyes and ears.

The arrangement had worked out well. Stanhope was an unimaginative but adequate CFO, who relied on long hours and hard work to compensate for his rather pedestrian intellect. He kept his eye on things, particularly the CEO, dutifully reporting anything he thought his master needed to know about and answering any of Manfort's questions about financial details and other goings on a board member would typically never hear about.

He preferred to think of these minions as his special protégés. Spy, however accurate, sounded vulgar. Not that vulgarity bothered Manfort in the least, but he enjoyed the way special protégé sounded, like the FBI's special agents. None of his special protégés knew about the others. And the great thing was that this espionage network cost him nothing. In fact, he had earned a reputation for helping his startups fill key positions as well as being a good mentor.

But now, Steve Stanhope was dead, and Khatri and Culpepper were making a power play to hire a new CFO. Just like that, he had no one inside Aztound Technologies.

Manfort had made good use of the intelligence Stanhope provided him. It enabled him to ask the kind of questions at board meetings that made Khatri believe Manfort had an uncanny, nearly prescient, insight into the issues Aztound was facing. That was obvious from Khatri's increasingly deferential behavior towards him, though not enough to overcome the CEO's obvious distaste for seeking advice from him or, for that matter, talking to him at all. Which suited Manfort just fine; it was part of why he had cultivated his abrasive, arrogant persona, to get people to stop pestering him about diddly shit. The other part was, he knew he *was* superior to most people, as evidenced by his financial success. Besides, he had been abrasive and arrogant long before he learned how to use those traits to his advantage. Might as well go with your strength.

Having the intelligence from Stanhope and buffing his reputation as an astute board member—valuable though that was in increasing the intimidation factor—had not been essential. Because Chet Khatri had turned out to be an excellent CEO. Manfort felt confident in the man's ability to drive a successful IPO. But that did not matter. Garrett Manfort had learned to never rely solely on his judgement of his companies' leaders. He had in the past been badly burned doing so. He'd had CEOs lie, cheat and steal, as well as display remarkable incompetence, all of which he could tolerate, so long as they made him money. Which he could best assure by knowing what they were up to. So Manfort believed in attaching an insurance policy, in the form of one or more special protégés, to all his companies, no exceptions. After all, that's what insurance was for: risk abatement.

In fact, at least one good thing had come out of the Stanhope mess: he would soon have a special protégé in place in one of his most recent investments, where he strongly suspected unacceptable management shenanigans. But right now he had to focus on shoring up Aztound Technologies.

Time to reel in a new sucker.

Chapter 13

Aztound Technologies may have treated Maddie decently financially, or at least offered to do so if she would sign their NDA, but that was where their benevolence ended.

The company had made it clear to Ed Wax and me that they were circling the wagons. We, on Maddie's behalf, would get no further information from them. No interviews. No documents or records of any kind. Not even a friendly chat. Direct all inquiries related to Steve Stanhope's death to their attorney.

We did. The lawyer's response was that we should direct all inquiries to the police, who in turn would not comment on an ongoing investigation, except for Detective Taylor's surreptitious off-the-record communication with me. And, the Aztound attorney had admonished us in writing, do not bother company staff. They had all been briefed on the situation and been reminded that their standard NDAs had draconian penalties for any such disclosures to outsiders.

Such obstinate obstruction did not deter Ed Wax.

Unmasked

Instead, it got his fighting juices flowing.

* * *

Maddie and I were again seated with Ed at the conference table in his office.

"Aztound Technologies won't help us in any way, at least not voluntarily," he said to Maddie by way of getting started. "But it seems clear that, to get the answers you want, let alone shake loose their money, we have to start where the murder took place. So I've prepared a wrongful death suit to force them to open the kimono. I just need your okay to file it."

Maddie looked perplexed. "Open the kimono?"

"Stop withholding information," I said, silently proud at the growth of my business jargon vocabulary, much of which I owed to meals with Nick Marchetti.

"What exactly is a wrongful death suit?"

"It's a civil suit claiming they were negligent in their duty of care to Steve," Ed said. "They had the legal obligation to safeguard his safety in the workplace."

Maddie thought a moment. "So we sue them, then they have to talk to us?"

"The judge can force them to," Ed said. "We can take depositions. Subpoena documents and other records. Make royal pains-in-the ass of ourselves."

Maddie nodded. "How much will we ask for?"

"We'll ask for $50 million. That'll get their attention."

Maddie did not bat an eye at that figure. "Will we win?"

"It's a longshot. But I doubt we'll ever see the inside of a courtroom. My bet is that they agree to a settlement. The publicity of a trial would be deadly for their IPO hopes. They'll want this to go away as quickly and quietly as possible."

"Let's do it," Maddie said.

A hush descended over our little conclave. Ed broke the silence, speaking directly to Maddie. "Please keep in mind, we started all of this to get to the truth about Steve's murder, not to get compensation. So don't get hung up on the 50 million, that's just a bargaining chip."

But it's like not thinking of purple. Once those dollar signs and all those zeros get in your head...

Chapter 14

Howard Penning sat in the booth at the pizza joint, took a bite from the first slice of his large pepperoni, and marveled at what had just transpired.

He had spent a depressing day orienting Deepa Patel, Aztound's new chief financial officer. It had been painful, because, once again, he had been passed over for CFO of a company he had served well and faithfully as controller, only to then have to teach his new boss the ropes.

At his CFO interview with Chet Khatri, Howie had dazzled his CEO with his detailed knowledge of Aztound's budget and expense numbers, all without referring to any reports, spreadsheets, or notes. He figured for sure he had aced the interview. Then Chet had called him in, told him he was a valued employee, his accounting knowledge was impressive, yadda, yadda, yadda. But they had chosen another candidate for chief financial officer, one who they felt had better finance experience and had successfully taken a company public. It was déjà vu bullshit.

Howie took a long draught from his mug of beer. He knew the real reason he hadn't gotten the promotion was that he didn't fit the image of a tech CFO. He was short, fat, and balding. Whereas this Patel woman was a real looker. It was appearance discrimination, pure and simple. Plus, Chet was probably screwing her, or planning to.

Howie added age discrimination to his list of grievances. Now 55, a lifelong bachelor, he had gotten his B.A. in accounting at Eastern New Mexico University, where he'd been a solid B-minus student, nearly 30 years ago. Now all they wanted in Silicon Valley were good-looking, over-achieving young, Stanford hotshots, barely out of college. And these over-educated Asians were clannish. Khatri had loaded the company with Indian staff, particularly those engineers and their support staff in Bangalore. He could barely understand some of them with their thick accents. Thankfully, this Patel woman didn't have one; it would have driven him nuts.

He had been at his desk brooding about all this injustice when he got the call from Garrett Manfort. He knew that Manfort was one of the board members. The man had asked to meet him in the parking garage at Santana row that evening. They sat together in Manfort's fancy car and had a great conversation. Manfort said he'd had his eye on Howard, had been aware that

Unmasked

Howard was responsible for the excellent financial reports Steve Stanhope provided to the board. It was a shame, he said, that others did not fully appreciate Howard's talents; though he had tried to sway them to promote Howard, he had been outvoted.

Manfort said he invested in a lot of companies and there would always be a place for a man like Howard in one of them. Of course, he hoped Howard would stay at Aztound Technologies and help grow the business. Howard could reap the rewards for all his hard work when his stock options soared after they went public. And Howard could help Manfort assure that happened by being his secret eyes and ears inside the company.

By the time Howie got out of what he knew was a six-figure Lincoln Navigator Black Label, their arrangement had been sealed. He was a committed special protégé, though that term had never been uttered. Had Garrett Manfort asked him to take an oath of allegiance, he would have done so willingly.

Basking in the afterglow, Howie drove to the pizza parlor in the strip mall near his condo and treated himself to a large. And pondered the fancy car he was certain would be in his future.

* * *

As Manfort drove away from Howard Penning, he laughed out loud. Recruiting the fat schmuck had been the proverbial piece of cake.

Manfort had been on the CFO hiring committee along with Culpepper and Chet Khatri. He had interviewed all the finalists Chet had selected. Chet had mentioned there was a lone internal candidate, Howard Penning, who had not made the cut. He was, Chet had said, a good accountant with limited leadership skills, little understanding of the broader business, and no experience managing a company's assets and liabilities or planning for future financial needs. And he presented poorly; you could never put the man in front of investors or analysts. Penning was an accounting soldier who knew all the numbers but had no idea what they meant, let alone how to spin them. He would forever be a controller.

Until that moment, Howard Penning had been just another of the faceless Aztound Technologies underlings. But Manfort's ears had perked up, because most of his special protégés were grunts in accounting and finance. They tended to have fewer job prospects and less self-confidence than other tech industry professionals, making them suckers for his pitch. They would toil away for years, content to feed him information in exchange for a few strokes and the thing they valued so highly, job security.

And these folks had access to the financial numbers for the entire business, the myriad details the board never saw. Numbers which spoke to Manfort like sheet music to a musician. *I know that I'd much rather spend quality time with a good spreadsheet than talk to people,* Manfort thought. *Probably why I'm such an asshole most of the time. That, and the sheer joy of intimidation. Though not when I'm handling one of my precious special protégés. Then I use the carrot, though when the stick is called for, well...*

Chapter 15

Chet Khatri sat in his corner office at Aztound Technologies, mindlessly approving invoices for payment. He used the services of a variety of business and management consultants and thus had to perform this weekly paperwork chore. Though it was all automated, so no actual paper, but still dreary work. Which he always zipped through as rapidly as possible. Click-click-click.

Working at his computer, Khatri was thinking about the crisis he was facing. Not the one that kept him up at night, the IPO, because, however desirable, getting that done was indeed a crisis. But at least what needed to be done for that was known. Whereas with the Stanhope mess, he had no playbook. But how he handled it could well be his defining test as CEO, certainly the most significant challenge he had yet faced in his career. Because the wrongful death lawsuit he had just reread could scuttle the IPO.

The spark that set it off had been Steve Stanhope's death. *That was a shame,* he thought, *but shit happens.* Problem was, like the Santa Ana winds, the flames had been fanned by his own knee-jerk defensiveness, supported by the similar instincts of both Culpepper and Manfort. This led to the warnings, direct and indirect, to all staff; minimal cooperation with the police; stonewalling Madison Stanhope and her lawyer and investigator; and generally callous treatment of Stanhope herself. All had led to yesterday's conflagration, the wrongful death suit.

That had finally gotten Khatri to acknowledge that what he had dismissed as an unpleasant incident, albeit extreme—though certainly not something he should allow to distract him—had become a full-blown crisis. Khatri admitted to himself that he had ignored other warning signs as well. Grumbling in the ranks about all the secrecy and the constant reminders about NDAs. Their questions about why the company was taking such a hard line with the authorities when one of their own had been murdered at his desk, and why the company had waited for this tragedy to beef up physical security.

Khatri had just finished his invoice approval tedium when his new executive assistant informed him that Myrna Marsh had arrived for their meeting. He checked the time. She was five minutes early. "Show her in."

Based in Los Angeles, Myrna Marsh was the country's premier corporate crisis management consultant, commanding commensurate fees. She had as close to a perfect record as you can get in a field where the results are subjective. Though they had never met, Khatri knew that Marsh was called "My way or the highway Myrna" for good reason.

As she entered, Khatri stood and greeted a short, thin woman of indeterminate middle age. She had salt and pepper hair pulled back in a tight bun, a pinched face, thin lips, and wore almost no makeup. And no jewelry whatsoever. Marsh was dressed in a nondescript navy-blue suit jacket and skirt, with a plain cream blouse. Unlike most diminutive businesswomen she wore flats.

Khatri walked over and extended his hand. "Chet Khatri. I'm pleased to meet you, Ms. Marsh."

Her small hand had a firm grip. When she spoke, she seemed to grow in stature. Her voice was deep and confident. "Good to meet you, too, Chet. Please call me Myrna."

They sat on comfortable chairs across a coffee table in a conversation area in a corner of Khatri's spacious office. "How was your flight?"

"Faster than a drive from almost anywhere to almost anywhere else in L.A. But we have no time to waste, Chet, so let's get to it."

"Okay."

"The biggest problem with crisis management is you first have to admit you have a crisis."

"That's why I called you," Khatri said. "I get it now.

Unmasked

I should have labelled this a crisis sooner. But I have people coming to me with their hair on fire over some dire emergency or another all the time." As he said it, Khatri felt foolish. Stanhope's murder was hardly like those run-of-the-mill issues, however dramatic.

Myrna raised an eyebrow, signaling that she too thought his remark was insensitive and inane. But she let it pass. "Don't beat yourself up. Most CEOs don't recognize when a true crisis has been ignited. They do a deny-minimize two-step, hoping to contain the damage and make the problem go away. It's like letting a little grass fire grow into a wildfire, something we're getting to know too much about. Anyway, all that matters is that you're there now."

"I am," Khatri said. He was also aware of all the overused fire metaphors. *Well, this is hell, so maybe they're appropriate.*

"Okay. First, some ground rules. Number 1: Don't listen to your lawyers. They're risk averse. Their main goal is to limit your exposure. They only think short-term, about the specific legal issues at hand. They can't and won't think strategically about the future of your business.

"You, on the other hand, are a risk taker. That's your job. Your main objectives now are to weather the storm, make sure there's no lasting damage, and have a successful IPO. Everything else is secondary."

Khatri nodded. *She gets it!*

"Now, you need to know that I too am a lawyer. Just a different kind, one aligned with your objectives. But keep in mind that Aztound Technologies is my client. The company has the full protection of attorney-client privilege. As do you for any actions done on behalf of the company in your role as CEO."

"That's good," Khatri said. He knew what Myrna had left unsaid. If he had done anything illegal beyond the scope of his duties, privilege did not apply.

"Which leads us to rule number two. I'm not a typical consultant. I'm not here to give advice. I'm here to tell you what to do. If we can't agree about something I want done, I'm out of here."

My way or the highway. "That's a tough one."

"Always is. CEOs hate to relinquish power and control. I can't make you do anything, but I can't help you if you won't stick to the program."

Khatri took a slow, deep breath and smiled ruefully. It was his job to get the IPO done. On this point, Manfort and Culpepper were in complete agreement. But would they buy Marsh's scheme? Culpepper would be reasonable, but Manfort would be a hard sell regardless of what the plan was, because being contrary was his default position. *Ah, well, who said being a CEO would be easy?*

"Okay, I understand."

"So, two simple rules. Don't listen to the other lawyers. Do listen to me. Now, have you signed my contract?"

Aztound's corporate counsel had already reviewed it. She wanted to make changes, but Khatri knew Marsh wouldn't accept them; he had already heard about those two damn rules. "Yes," he said, handing her a signed copy. "It sure was short and sweet."

It was Myrna Marsh's turn to smile. "That's me."

Chapter 16

Culpepper and Khatri knew better than to wear masks at a meeting with Manfort unless they wanted to deal with an extended rant. At least he, like them, was fully vaccinated.

By the time they met that evening in Khatri's office, Culpepper and Manfort had read the lawsuit and Chet's outline of the key points in Myrna Marsh's plan. The high-level objectives were straightforward. First, settle the wrongful death lawsuit before it saw the light of day and got publicity. Second, do everything possible to help the police solve Steve Stanhope's murder as soon as possible. He and Marsh had fleshed out details for each of those objectives.

Culpepper led off, complimenting Chet for getting the renowned Myrna Marsh involved within hours of learning about the lawsuit. He agreed with the plan and was in favor of leaving the details to the CEO.

Manfort characteristically disagreed.

They were being pussies, Manfort thundered. Man-up and fight back. Get their high-priced lawyers and those from their insurance company to crush this frivolous lawsuit.

Couldn't they find evidence that Stanhope, like any startup CFO worth his salt, had turned down budget requests for improved physical security at corporate headquarters? (*They could,* Chet thought.) And hadn't Stanhope himself spearheaded the widespread use of stringent NDAs in the company? (*He had,* Chet admitted to himself.) Blame the victim, goddammit! It was the American way.

And, speaking of pussies, he would be damned if he would let Ugly Myrna dictate what they did. (Chet later learned that the two had crossed swords before and Marsh had gotten the better of Manfort.)

It was Culpepper who had talked Manfort down. He pointed out that the lawsuit had been filed by Ed Wax, whoever the hell he was, along with famed Silicon Valley attack-dog attorney Annie Oakley, a detail the impatient Manfort had missed when he had skimmed the complaint.

Culpepper calmly outlined the nightmare PR scenario. Oakley would likely spin it as the tale of a poor widow and her children abandoned and mistreated by a heartless corporation, forced to sue to get what they rightfully deserved. All they wanted was an explanation of what had happened to their beloved husband and father and just compensation for the corporate irresponsibility that had led to his death. "What," she'll ask, "are they trying to hide?"

"Think about the impact, Garrett," Culpepper said evenly. "On investors. On the investment bankers. On financial analysts and pundits. Think about Annie Oakley denouncing us on CNN, Fox and the cable business news networks. Aztound will be crucified. You can kiss your precious IPO goodbye."

That was exactly what Khatri had been thinking about. Sure, his last startup had been successful, but that liquidity event had been a sale to one of the tech superpowers. He had personally made millions, but now his sights were set on billions. That served to focus his attention.

"Greg's right. I was on a conference call with the investment banks this afternoon. Their bottom line is, either we get this Stanhope thing behind us fast or the IPO is off indefinitely. I didn't even mention the lawsuit. I think if they knew about it, they'd kill the IPO now."

In the end, Manfort capitulated. Financial self-interest carried the day. "Do what you have to do," he barked at Khatri. He wagged a finger at him. "You're responsible for cleaning up this mess. You own it now. It's your ass on the line. And I don't want to hear any more about Ugly Myrna."

* * *

Unmasked

That evening, Manfort was thinking about Nick Marchetti. He heard through the VC grapevine that Marchetti had been asking around about Aztound Technologies.

Manfort's buddy said that Marchetti did not seem to be after anything in particular, just doing the kind of casual information gathering Silicon Valley investors routinely did, more like gossiping to keep abreast with the fast-paced technology sector. But Manfort thought the timing was curious, what with the IPO on the horizon. Was Marchetti interested in investing in a mezzanine round prior to the IPO? Was his billionaire pal Mike Gold a possible investor as well? Getting their endorsement could seal the deal for a successful public offering.

If he was honest with himself, he had to admit that he respected Culpepper and Khatri standing up to him about the new CFO. Deepa Patel *was* a better choice than the guy he had been backing, a long-time special protégé but a plodder. Of course, he would never admit that to them, any more than he would that they had been right to pressure him on quickly resolving the beef with Stanhope's widow and getting that whole nasty business behind them.

It was another reminder to keep his eye on the ball, not let anger and pride take over. When combined, he knew, they often resulted in his acting stubborn and belligerent, overriding sound business judgement, ultimately costing him money.

Which was unforgivable.

Chapter 17

"It appears that our little lawsuit made Chet Khatri and his brain trust see the light. As well as fear of Annie Oakley."

We were once more seated around the table in Ed's office. "Who," Maddie said, "is Annie Oakley?"

"Annie Oakley is one of Silicon Valley's top attorneys. She's smart, quick-thinking and tenacious. Usually wins, and even when she loses, leaves her opponents bruised and beaten. She's the model for those aggressive, beautiful, sharp-tongued female lawyers you see on TV and in the movies. Only Annie makes up her brilliant legal arguments and snide comebacks on the fly, not reading lines from some writer's carefully crafted script. She scares the pants off people."

"What's she got to do with us?"

Ed grinned. "I added Annie's name as your litigant along with mine. She let me do it as a favor, no charge. She owes me. My hunch was that was all we would need from her. I was right. Khatri specifically said I should, and I quote, 'call her off.'"

"You said they caved," I said. "What exactly does that mean?"

"They're desperate for us to withdraw the suit before news of it becomes public." Ed turned to Maddie. "Here's their proffer." He read from handwritten notes on a legal pad.

"Point One: You get the balance of your husband's annual salary and that bonus they promised in one lump sum.

"Point Two: All of Steve's stock options will be fully vested retroactively.

"Point Three: Their liability insurance carrier will pay you $4.9 million in exchange for a release from future claims. Somehow not going over $5 million was important to them, don't ask me why. And the release is standard practice.

"Point Four: They'll cooperate fully with us on the investigation, within reason.

"Point Five: Khatri promised to, as he coyly put it, correct the miscommunication with his staff about cooperating with the police."

Ed looked up. "Questions?"

Curious investigator that I am, I jumped right in. "How much are the stock options worth?"

Maddie was quick to reply. "Aztound issued options once a year with five-year vesting schedules. Steve got more each year. They total 200,000 shares. The IPO is expected to price at around $16. The average strike price is two bucks. Pretax net is $2.8 million."

I was impressed. Maddie sure had mastered those figures. She had said she managed their money and did it well; I could understand why.

"It could be a lot more if you hold on and the stock takes off," Ed said.

Maddie nodded. "A hell of a lot more. But can't we hold out for more now?" She clearly still had that $50 million figure in her head.

"Chet Khatri was frank," Ed said. "The main reason they're mending their ways—again, his words—is that they want to announce the IPO soon and our lawsuit is a potential stumbling block. Which was what we were counting on.

"He's aligning your interests with his. Your opportunity for the big payday is a successful IPO. If they give you a big payoff now, they lose leverage to assure your good behavior."

Maddie looked puzzled.

"He means you won't badmouth them," I said.

That she understood. "Okay. So when do I get the salary and bonus and insurance checks?"

"I'll make sure the agreement says funds disburse at signing."

I had more questions. "What does 'cooperate fully within reason' mean?"

"Yeah, well, it does sound like a contradiction. The

actual wording will be more explicit. All it means is that we can't go fishing for things that are trade secrets or have nothing to do with what we're investigating. That can be vague, but we lawyers will get it worded so it's workable. There's boilerplate language we can copy from similar agreements. Let me worry about that."

"When will this new spirit of cooperation start?" I said.

"If Maddie agrees, we should get this buttoned up tomorrow, day after at worst. They're highly motivated to have that lawsuit withdrawn."

After a bit more discussion, Maddie agreed.

Chapter 18

I cleverly deduced that Aztound Technologies was not waiting for the completion of the legal agreement to turn over a new leaf with the police. The clue was what Detective Bart Taylor had just said to me over the phone as I drove back to my office.

"It seems Aztound Technologies is turning over a new leaf and cooperating with us now, Joe."

"That's good news," I said.

"Their CEO apologized for what he termed 'misunderstandings from misguided but well-meaning staff.' Like who, himself? He even suggested we pool our efforts, that it was in everyone's best interest to solve the Stanhope murder as soon as possible."

"Was I part of that 'we'?"

"Yeah, can you believe it? Gave me and my partner a good laugh."

"I thought you guys were homed in on Santiago."

"Still some loose ends. You know how that is."

Right. Like did our client order a hit. "Are you and I also now cooperating?"

"In the usual way. You learn anything useful, you tell me."

"Sort of takes the 'co' out of cooperating." I said,

"That's how *we* operate," Bart said, and ended the call.

Nothing new about that. Still, he had slipped me the information about the murder weapon, though I still wasn't sure why.

* * *

"Bart can share," I said to Sally, "but he does his best to disguise it, lest they take away his cop secret decoder ring."

"Lest?"

"It's a long story."

Sally and I were seated at my desk. She was between classes at her studio across the hall, where she taught self-defense.

"You going to open that package?"

"Sure." The package was from India. I opened it.

"That's a wicked-looking dagger, Joe."

It was about a foot long. "Technically, it's a letter opener."

"Huh?"

"It's the same model that was used to kill Steve Stanhope."

"The case you're working?"

"Yeah." I handed it to her, told her about Honorable Swordworks, their past and present business, and that this was a replica dagger sold as a classy souvenir letter opener in India.

She pointed to the guard, the part between the blade and the handle, and then the pommel, which is the endcap of the handle. "Are these real gold?"

"Gold plated."

"Snazzy," Sally said. She played a bit with it. "Also hefty." She tried to bend the shiny steel blade, unsuccessfully. "Got a nice, solid feel to it. But unbalanced. Most of the weight is in the blade."

"Longer than your typical letter opener," I said.

"If the blade wasn't so dull, this would make a fine weapon," Sally said, holding it by the handle, more like a sword than a knife.

Watching Sally gave me an idea. "Would you say people from India are smaller on average than most Americans?"

Sally nodded. "On average, yeah."

"And during the colonial period in India, British soldiers were smaller than now?"

"People are getting taller in general, so, yeah to that too."

"And hand size sort of goes along with height? And women tend to have smaller hands than men, even when they're the same height."

"Enough, Joe. What are you getting at?"

I pointed to Sally's hand, still holding the handle of the letter opener. "You're shorter than me by several inches, and your hand just fits that handle."

"So?"

"Stand up and try holding it like you want to stab someone sitting in front of you in the back."

Sally changed her grip. Her hand completely engulfed the rubber-covered haft, the part between the guard and the pommel. She held the letter opener at shoulder height and chopped down at the air in front of her. Then she changed her grip and tried it underhand.

"The weight helps when you're stabbing down," she said.

Which was not my point but was an interesting observation. "Let's go to the market," I said. "I have a craving for watermelon."

Sally gave me her "you're really losing it now" look, one I'd had the privilege of seeing all too often.

"Come on, indulge me."

Twenty minutes later, Sally and I returned from the little produce market down the block with a big watermelon. I'd have preferred a pumpkin, but it was the wrong season.

I had explained what I had in mind to Sally during our little outing, and I think she was intrigued. Though she wouldn't act like it.

Unmasked

I cleared my desk and spread newspaper over it. Positioned the watermelon in the middle of the desk. Took the letter opener in my right hand, raised my arm and stabbed down, overhand. The letter opener bounced off the watermelon.

"Now you try it," I said, handing Sally the letter opener.

She did. The sharp point of the letter opener easily pierced the skin and went deep inside. Sally let go. The watermelon had a knife stuck in its back.

We tried the experiment a few more times. Sally succeeded in assassinating the watermelon every time. I failed several more times before I mastered the technique that I had to use to control the letter opener with my bigger hand around the pommel as well as the hilt.

"So I'm a gifted athlete and you're a klutz."

"Maybe," I said. "Or maybe someone with a small hand can use this thing better than someone with a big hand."

"You mean, it's all about the grip?"

"This is a replica of a weapon made by Indians for British soldiers 150 years ago. By people with smaller hands, for people with smaller hands."

"Smaller than your bozo hands, that's for sure."

"I don't think six feet is particularly tall for an American man and my hands aren't big for my height."

"But you don't deny being a bozo?"

"Sticks and stones. Look, as you so astutely observed, in a hand with a good grip, the weight and gravity help the letter opener penetrate."

"So you don't need a lot of strength," she said, getting serious.

"Which makes it more likely the killer was a woman," I said.

"Or a smaller man," Sally said. "Or someone with a big hand who had practiced."

"Granted. But the strength required to penetrate ribs would normally make you think the killer was a man. I know I assumed that. We've just broadened the pool of suspects."

"Don't you want to narrow it?"

"Always a good thing," I agreed, "as long as you don't myopically eliminate the real killer."

Sally had to leave to lead a class. After all that work, I needed a pick-me-up. The watermelon had been severely trashed, and I didn't much care for watermelon anyway. It was time to head downstairs. Donut and smoothie time.

Chapter 19

Ed Wax was right, Aztound Technologies was highly motivated to get our lawsuit dropped. He texted me the next morning: **Deal signed. Suit dropped. Meet Khatri his office 1:30.**

As I headed out, I was thinking about the watermelon experiment. The watermelon rind was easy to penetrate once the letter opener went through the skin. A human back was another story. I looked it up. Three layers of muscle and other stuff, especially those ribs, were between the skin of the back and the heart. It was a lot to get through.

More, although the point was sharp, the letter opener had a dull blade. In order to go between those ribs and reach the heart, I was pretty sure it would have to enter with the blade horizontal, not vertical. But both Sally and I had oriented the blade vertically, it was the natural way to hold it, regardless of whether you were stabbing up or down.

Maybe the killer hadn't luckily missed the ribs. Maybe they had known exactly what they were doing, stabbing with the blade horizontal at exactly the right spot to slip between the ribs. HIPAA be damned, where was the autopsy report when I needed it?

It would remain my unmet lament.

* * *

The corporate headquarters of Aztound Technologies was in a free-standing, one-story building surrounded by a parking lot in an office park in San Jose. It was a lot smaller than I had expected. I parked in a visitor space in front.

Carrying my infrequently used attaché case to enhance my professional aura, I walked through the front door into a small lobby that appeared to have been recently refurbished. Everything looked new, from the furnishings to the light fixtures to the ceiling tiles to the paint on the walls. A young woman and a uniformed male security guard sat behind a built-in counter. The receptionist asked me if she could help me.

I gave her my card and said I had a meeting with Mr. Khatri at 1:30. She asked to see a photo ID but did not ask me to lower my mask so she could really see my face. She glanced at my driver's license, copied the number into a loose-leaf notebook, had me sign in, entered something into her computer and gave me a stick-on badge that said VISITOR. While the rent-a-cop checked the contents of my attaché case—a couple of pens, some breath mints, and my handy little notebook—she picked up the phone, tapped a button, and said, "Mr. Khatri's 1:30 is here."

I was ten minutes early and about to take a seat when a woman came through the inside door, which had a banner above it that proclaimed, "Prepare to be Aztounded!" I tried to get her name from the badge hung around her neck, but the print was too small for me to see without staring awkwardly at her chest. "Please come with me, Mr. Brink."

We went through the door, which automatically closed behind us, made a left turn, walked past a closed door to what I would later learn had been Steve Stanhope's office, then to the corner where there was another closed office door. My escort offered me the chair next to her desk just outside that door. I detected it was Chet Khatri's office based on the sign next to the doorway that read Chet Khatri, Chief Executive Officer.

"He'll just be a minute," she said. "May I get you something to drink?"

Grateful for the excuse to unmask, I sipped my Diet Coke. Moments later, the office door opened and a man also holding an open can of soda made eye contact with me as he approached. I stood. He extended his hand. "Mr. Brink? I'm Chet Khatri. Welcome to Aztound Technologies."

Khatri had a large corner office. The two outside walls had wide windows with uninspiring views of the front and side parking lots. There were no pictures on the other two walls. One was filled by a large whiteboard, the other with a large banner that read, "Aztound 'Em!"

We sat at a small conference table. Khatri took a seat at one end. I sat two seats away along the side at his right.

"Thanks for coming on such short notice, Joe." *First names are so chummy!*

"My pleasure, Chet." *I've only been trying to see you for a week.*

Adopting a face that struggled to strike a balance between mournful and helpful, he went on, "Now that the liability thing has been resolved, the insurance company and our lawyers will finally let me talk to you. I want to assure you, we're anxious to get to the bottom of this tragedy."

As, yes, pity the poor CEO, a helpless victim of his advisors. "That's all Mrs. Stanhope wants," I said.

I had called ahead and given Khatri's executive assistant—not a mere admin, I was informed—presumably the same woman with the indecipherable name badge who had escorted me inside—a rundown of what I hoped to accomplish during my visit. Khatri and I chatted a few minutes. I asked the usual questions. He gave me bland answers. Said he had noticed nothing unusual about Steve Stanhope's behavior or demeanor leading up to his murder. He knew of no one with a

Unmasked

grudge against Steve, who was as well liked as a CFO, the man whose job was often to say no, could be. No threats. No rivalries. Solid citizen. Shocked that anyone would do him harm.

"What was Steve like?"

"The dress code here is pretty loose," Chet said. He was wearing a light blue golf shirt, tan Dockers, and loafers. "But Steve always was just a bit better dressed than anyone else. Guys rarely bring a sport coat; he always wore one, though it usually ended up hung behind his door. It was the image he felt a CFO should convey. That carried over to his general demeanor. Serious but pleasant. Businesslike." He smiled. "Our adult supervision."

Khatri said that Steve routinely worked late, especially during closings. This fiscal year-end was particularly crucial, as it would be followed by an IPO filing; they were looking to go public in about six months. For the first time, they would be exposing their financial results to the public. The pressure on everyone involved was immense.

Unprompted, Khatri admitted that their security had been lax. He took full responsibility for that, he said, but a startup must be frugal. In any case, they were correcting their security shortcomings even as we spoke. They now had RFID badges for everyone; that would provide a log of comings and goings and control access more granularly. A security guard was on duty

24/7. New cameras were being installed everywhere. *Too bad it had taken an employee's murder to make that happen.* "Were you here when the body was discovered?"

He shook his head sadly. "I'd been in San Francisco meeting with investment bankers late the night before. Stayed over for another round of meetings the next day. Of course, that got cancelled when the call came about Steve."

San Francisco was just an hour away, plenty close enough for him to have made the round trip and committed the murder.

Letting me know he was a busy man with big, important things to attend to, and that I had gotten my allotted portion of his precious CEO time, Khatri stood. "I apologize, Mr. Brink, but I'm really jammed up today. And I just don't think I have anything else useful for you myself."

I stayed seated. Khatri seemed taken aback by my lack of deference. When the king rises, everyone rises. I fed his discomfort by letting the awkwardness linger a couple of beats, then said, "I see you've replaced Mandy."

Seemingly puzzled, he said, "Who?"

"Mandy. Amanda Aparicio."

"Oh. Well, yes, Amanda was a valued employee. She'd been guarding the gate for Steve and me since we started the company. But the shock of finding him like that, it's understandable that she wanted to leave, make a new start somewhere else. We were glad to help.

"Now, I really must attend to other things. I arranged for our office manager to spend some time with you, show you whatever you want to see, that sort of thing. Mary Jo knows more about this place than anyone."

Chapter 20

Mary Jo Hart was barely five feet tall if that and looked to be about 60, with a lot of gray in her dark hair. She had a kind, intelligent face, and a ready smile. After making the introductions, Chet herded us out and closed his office door behind us.

"Where would you like to start?"

"I'd like to get a sense of the physical layout," I said.

"Sure. How about we walk around outside first?"

As we headed to the lobby, I said, "Who handles security?"

"Physical security is one of my many jobs. I didn't pay much attention to it before. It's front burner now. As you'll see, the upgrade is still underway."

"What about that night?"

She told me all the alarms, locks and security cameras in the old system had been working, as well as the window sensors. The company that monitored the security system confirmed that, and that there had been no breaches.

"Was there a patrol?"

Unmasked

"Yes. Of course, now we have 24/7 guard coverage onsite. Anyway, they did a drive-through a few times a night. Started around 11 p.m. They made no report of unusual activity. In all the time we've been here, they never have."

We went out through the lobby and stood in front, of the building. We started walking along the sidewalk between the building and the parking area that surrounded it. There were two trucks in the parking lot from a security company, and workers on ladders were installing cameras and other equipment on and around the building.

"We got the basic system up two weeks ago. Now they're adding more cameras and whatnot. When this is done, we'll have excellent coverage. Including the parking lot."

Like locking the barn door after the horse is stolen. Along the side of the building, we passed a windowless door. "Is this a fire door?"

"Yes. Same on the other side. Always locked, no entrance, exit with the crash bar on the inside, not to be used except in an emergency. Alarm goes off when open. The locks and alarms were functioning properly that night, I tested them myself the next day. So did the police. And no fire doors or windows were opened."

Around the rear, there was another door with a reinforced window and a sign that read "employees only, visitors please use front entrance."

"This door and the front door are the employee entrances," Hart said. "They both lock automatically outside regular work hours; you can get out but not in, but lots of people had keys. We changed the locks after the incident, restricted who has keys. As soon as the new system is fully functional, the new badges will act as keys and control all access."

The incident? Then again, what else should they call it? Like saying passed away instead of died. Still, it seemed somehow disrespectful to the man who had lost his life at his desk.

"How about the roof?"

"It's a low building, so it's easy to get on the roof. And there's space between the roof and the dropped ceiling. But the only way in is through a hatch up there that's always been locked and alarmed. And it also was not opened."

We went inside through the unlocked employee backdoor, into a sea of cubicles. "This door is unlocked from 6 a.m. until 8 p.m. But like I said, it'll be badge controlled in a few days."

"The building is smaller than I expected."

"Our R&D staff is all in Bangalore. This location is mostly sales and marketing, accounting and finance, and professional services. And people are working from home more now. So we need less office space as we grow than before hybrid work caught on."

The tall cubicles were sure beehive-like, but there

was no buzz of activity. More like the soft click-clack of keyboards and the sound of muted voices.

"How many people work at this location?"

"About 100, give or take, although less than half of them come to the office on any given day. Another 50 or so are in Seattle; we acquired a cloud security company there last year. And a couple of hundred in Bangalore, mostly engineers.

We had walked the length of the cubehive back to the front offices. Hart offered me a seat in her small office and asked if I'd like something to drink. I had her point me to the men's room. When I returned, she had two cold cans of Diet Coke. As I sat, she closed the door.

We each opened our can and took a sip.

"Do you have any way of knowing who else besides Steve Stanhope was in the building that night?"

"If you mean when he was killed, no one except for the murderer," Hart said.

"How do you know?"

"The old cameras produced lousy video, but we caught the killer coming and going. Let me show you."

Which I already knew from Bart. I had been waiting to see if Hart would volunteer the information before I broached the subject.

As she worked at her computer to bring up the video, she said, "I spent a couple of hours watching the front and back door footage and tracking people entering and leaving. At least I had logs of when the doors opened and closed so I could skip through dead time. But trying to figure out who was who was painstaking, especially with some wearing masks and the crappy image quality and lighting.

"Here we are. The last staff and the janitor had left the building by 9:20 p.m. Except for Steve, of course. Then this."

I stood behind Amanda and watched the screen. There was a shot from the camera over the back entrance. The timestamp read 10:22 p.m. She clicked the play button.

The video quality was poor. A fuzzy figure wearing a hoodie pulled low over their face came into the picture, opened the door with a key and entered. The door closed behind them. She played it again in slow motion.

"Do you recognize them?"

"No," she said. "I can't tell if it's a man or woman, can you?"

"I can't even guess at their build, let alone gender," I said. "Those clothes could be tight or loose."

"Did you notice the gloves?"

"I did," I said. "And it looks like they're wearing a mask along with the hoodie."

Hart advanced the video to 10:31 p.m. What appeared to be the same person exited the building, again keeping their face turned away from the camera, which was easy when they were walking away.

"So, there's our killer," I said. "Maybe the cops were

able to enhance the video."

"If they did, we haven't heard about it. I had one of our IT wizards play with it. He said the resolution was too low; enhancing it made it even more blurred due to pixilation, whatever that means."

"May I have a copy?"

"I'll have to check about that and get back to you."

"I understand. Are there any interior cameras?"

Hart shook her head. "Not then. But there are now."

Big help. "I wish we knew the ME's estimated time of death," I said, thinking out loud. "Although it probably wouldn't help much. Unless the body is still warm, the best they can get from it is usually a window of a few hours. Unless they've got some other evidence to narrow it down."

"Like this video?"

"Yes, exactly like that. But we have a nine-minute window. You already said you have no record of who had keys, right?"

"Not that's accurate. We've handed out a lot of them over the years and don't always get them back when someone leaves. To tell the truth, the record keeping was pretty sloppy, particularly in the early days. And the keys are easy to copy. Also, sometimes people lost them, but we never bothered to rekey. Until now."

"So knowing they used a key doesn't narrow the pool of suspects," I said. "It must have been a relief when the police named the janitor as their prime suspect."

"It helped keep the staff from getting paranoid that one of us was the killer. He's on the tape coming in at the usual time, about 7 o'clock. Let me show you."

She positioned the tape. It showed a man wearing a mask but no hoodie entering at 6:58 p.m.

"You recognize him?"

"No. They're just the janitors, you know? And they keep changing personnel. Could have been the person we saw come in later, but I sure couldn't say that for sure." She skipped ahead. The man emerged at 10:02 p.m.

"So, three hours," I said.

"Usually there are two of them and they're done in under two hours. There's usually not that much to do. Empty wastebaskets, clean and resupply the restrooms, that sort of thing."

"I don't suppose any of the cameras showed cars coming and going."

"No, they only covered the front and back entrances."

"I don't remember seeing any fencing anywhere," I said.

"There isn't any. It would be easy to walk in from the street or the buildings next door or in the back. There's just a row of low hedges separating the parking lots.

No wonder they had fallen all over themselves to settle the wrongful death suit. I wondered how their insurance company let them get away with such a vulnerable setup.

We talked some more. I went through the same questions I had asked Khatri. She didn't bat an eye when I asked about her alibi; she was home with her husband from about 6 p.m. Otherwise, her answers were similar to Khatri's. She also verified that, except for Amanda Aparicio, no Aztound employees in the United States had left the company since Steve's murder. I had been hoping someone had suspiciously bailed, but no such luck.

Now I knew what Detective Taylor had meant by his reference to the video of the Candice Hubbard murder and his cryptic comment about hating it when that happens. Only that was high quality video and the killer's face had been clear. And even so, it had led to the wrong suspect.

Chapter 21

The last thing I wanted to accomplish on this visit was to see Steve Stanhope's office. It was the one with the closed door next to Khatri's.

As we walked over, Hart said, "Thank goodness they let us take down that yellow tape. Anyway, we're not using the office. Who wants to work where someone died?" She pointed down the corridor past the lobby door. "I put the new CFO down there in what had been a conference room."

Hart said that other than having been cleaned—the cops left their usual mess, especially fingerprint powder—the office remained as it had been. Except for Steve's laptop, which the police had confiscated. And, of course, the letter opener. Other than that, she had boxed up Steve's personal effects for his wife.

Hart unlocked the door, mentioning that all the executives had offices that locked with their own keys. We stood just inside the doorway. I sensed Hart was reluctant to go further inside.

Stanhope's office was about half the size of Khatri's.

Unmasked

A table faced the office door, a desk behind faced the windows. On the desk sat a large monitor, a keyboard and what I thought was a printer. I pointed towards where a section of carpet about three feet square had been cut out between the desk and the table, presumably removed by the police where the blood had stained it. "Is that where Steve was sitting?"

Still in the doorway, Hart nodded. "Steve kept his laptop on the table. He liked to work facing the door. He could also turn around and use the big screen and keyboard on the desk, connected wirelessly to the laptop."

I took out my phone and snapped a few photos. I pictured Steve sitting, hunched over his laptop, working. But I could only conjure up a vague image of the killer behind him, holding the letter opener, preparing to strike the fatal blow. Oh, for psychic powers!

"Do you have any idea what specifically he was working on that night?"

"Most likely year-end stuff. Steve was a neatnik and a bit anal about not using paper. He wanted everything electronic. Never printed anything; that's a high-speed scanner next to the monitor, he used it to convert paper to files."

"What about his phone?"

"The cops took that, too."

"Was anything missing?"

"Not that I know of."

"Where did Steve keep the letter opener?"

She pointed. "Next to the monitor. It was a gift from Chet, you know, from a trip to Bangalore. I don't think Steve ever used it to open mail, but he liked to fiddle with it. He always did that when he told you he was cutting your budget. Other times, to make you worry he might. It was his little joke."

"I understand Mandy found the body."

"Mandy? You mean Amanda?"

"Sorry, my mistake."

"Amanda was always in early, like me. That day was no different. She ran to my office right away, nearly hysterical. I came over here, saw Steve, but didn't go inside. I stationed myself in the doorway while she called 9-1-1. Stayed there until the cops arrived. While I waited for them, I snapped a few photos with my phone. Let me show you."

She took her phone out of her pocket, found the photo she wanted and handed the phone to me. Steve sits in a chair behind the table, facing the door, the top of his head towards the camera, his face on the laptop keyboard. From the angle the shot was taken, he looks asleep. The letter opener can't be seen.

"I held the camera higher for the next one."

I swiped. Now the letter opener was visible, its handle protruding from Steve's back just to the left of his spine. As I had anticipated, the blade was turned horizontally.

"Those were the only ones I took," she said.

I handed back the phone. "Would you send them to me?"

"Same answer. I have to check with the powers that be first."

Trying to act like it was an afterthought, I said, "Tell me, what was Amanda Aparicio like? I mean, in general, not that day."

"She's a topnotch executive assistant, smart and efficient. Wicked sense of humor. Always kidding around and wisecracking. Kind of unfiltered. But not with outsiders, she was very professional when it was called for. We were both here when the company started. I really miss her."

Chapter 22

Roxie Roxbury was amused by how Chet Khatri fussed over each of his consultants. She had to set up their accounts for them, as if it were beneath them to do it themselves like all the other vendors managed to do. Then she would handhold them through a demo of how to submit an invoice, which any fool could figure out. She knew it was because Chet himself was an inept user. Go figure: a tech CEO intimidated by technology.

Roxie also got a kick out of how uncomfortable Chet had looked the other day when he brought Myrna Marsh to her cube, like he had made a wrong turn and found himself in an unfamiliar and potentially unsavory neighborhood. And the way he stumbled over Roxie's name when he introduced her, like it was a strain to retrieve it from his memory and he wasn't so sure he got it right; she was one of the practically nameless little people. He appeared visibly relieved when he retreated to the safety of executive row.

* * *

Unmasked

Just before she packed up to head home, Roxie thought about recent developments.

This Myrna Marsh that Chet had spent the better part of the afternoon with was some sort of crisis management consultant. Roxie knew that because she had entered it into the system when she set up Marsh's vendor account. And the guy Mary Jo was escorting around the building wasn't another security contractor, which Roxie had at first assumed. His name was Joe Brink; his company was Brink Investigations. She knew that from the security log she'd peaked at when she stopped by to schmooze with the receptionist and security guy. Or what passed for schmoozing with Roxie. Aztound did not get many visitors. Brink's had been the last entry.

Roxie looked up Joe Brink Investigations and learned he was a local private investigator. What, she wondered, was he up to? She would worm something about Brink out of Mary Jo. Though she did not say much herself, Roxie was a great listener, adept at getting people to gossip with her, especially a Chatty Kathy like Mary Jo Hart.

Roxie went over to check on her plant. It was neither thirsty nor curious about Marsh or Brink. She scolded the plant. Roxie loved Aztound Technologies. She had found a home here and she would do anything to protect it. The plant did not appreciate how good they had it here.

A crisis management consultant and a PI. She wondered if both had something to do with Steve Stanhope's murder. She would have to talk to Mary Jo about why they were there. People had been squirrely since that night. Roxie wanted things to settle back down.

Okay, plant, how do we make that happen?

Chapter 23

Amanda Aparicio never made it to Aspen.

She had gotten close. It had been snowing heavily; the vehicle had winter tires but no chains. Airbags and a seatbelt had not protected the driver from the drop into the gulch after the SUV apparently skidded off the highway rounding a curve at high speed. The police were calling it an accident.

I heard about this tragedy from Amanda's daughter Melanie. It was unclear why she had chosen to call me with the news. She was barely coherent, understandable under the circumstances.

As best I could tell, the accident had only been covered locally, in the Aspen area. Other than the garbled account from Melanie, I got what I knew by pulling up those reports online.

My PI brain reminded me not to assume everything portrayed as facts in the news was completely accurate. My experience with the news media was that they often got some things wrong in early reporting, then those mistakes were picked up and repeated until they effectively became truths. In any case, the squirrelly feeling I had gotten from Amanda Aparicio, her apparent deceptions, had me considering flying to Colorado to find out for myself.

Don't fly off half-cocked, I thought. I decided to first try calling the Colorado investigator who handled the accident. I wondered if I then flew off, would I be full-cocked?

My wit made me feel giddy. It was mid-morning, I'd had a longer-than-usual run, skipped second breakfast, then received the alarming news about Amanda. I needed fortification. Ten minutes later, I was back from picking up a couple of donuts and a smoothie downstairs. Not for the first time, I marveled at the strategic location of my office.

A few mouthfuls of donut did wonders to dampen my impulsiveness. I texted Bart Taylor, asking if he had heard about Amanda Aparicio's demise and if so, what he knew about it. He quickly replied: **Sucks when you know something like that before I do. Back to you soon.**

I replied: **I shared as soon as I heard.** I resisted adding an emoji.

* * *

While I was waiting to hear back from Bart, Ricky came into the office and sat across from me.

"I just finished talking to the owner of the janitorial service. It's a two-person office, this guy and his wife. They seem to spend all their time dealing with staffing problems. While I was there, she was either on the phone trying to track someone down or switching around people's assignments.

"Anyway, the guy told me that they had almost gone under during COVID when their customers closed their offices. Now things are slowly coming back. But he can't find enough people to work. We're talking minimum wage. Those that have the jobs desperately need them but move on as soon as something better turns up. And when they quit, they often just don't show up. No notice."

"What about our guy?"

"Javier Santiago," Ricky said, referring to his little notebook. "Been there a couple of months. No issues. Showed up on time, did his work, no complaints from customers. That is, before this thing. Anyway, they usually have at least two people at each job. It's for security. Also tends to keep them from stealing stuff. But being short staffed, Santiago was doing the route on his own. Which he completed around 4 a.m. They log the times on an app."

Ricky's notes agreed with the Aztound timeline I'd noted from the security video.

"What about his next job?"

"That was at one of those outfits that rent individual

offices short term. It's just down the street from Aztound. He got there at 10:10, left at 1:15."

"According to the app," I said.

"I should check if they have security footage to confirm that, huh?"

"Hold off. I'll see if the cops already did that."

"Speaking of cops, they came by looking for Santiago the next day. No one had heard from him, and he never showed up for work again."

"Did you ask how big he was?"

"Yeah, I remembered you told me to do that. The guy said he was about average for a Mexican man, a couple of inches shorter than himself. I figure about five-six. And medium build."

So he'd probably pass the watermelon test.

Ricky closed his notebook. "I made a copy of the photo they have on file and got the address and phone number they have for him. I guess I should visit the address next, right?"

"Sounds like a plan," I said.

"They mentioned one other thing. A lot of these folks are undocumented or have had skirmishes with the law before. Said they tend to bolt at any hint of suspicion about anything. And they seem to have a real good early warning system."

As he left, Ricky swiped my second donut.

* * *

"They're taking a closer look at it," Bart said. He was not big on greetings.

"Because of your persuasive charm?"

"Because until I called, the Colorado guy had no idea about the connection to a murder case. Same reason I didn't hear about Aparicio's death until you called me."

Bart went on to explain that the section of mountain highway Amanda went off was treacherous and accidents, sometimes fatal, were not unusual, especially for tourists unfamiliar with the conditions. "He said they have lots of signs, but what good are they in a blizzard or at night? Said it wouldn't be a bad thing if this makes some noise, could get guardrails bumped up on the highway department's list."

"How are you liking Santiago now?" I said.

"Until I have a better suspect, he's still it. Taking off like that is a sign of guilt."

"And you know most often it's just the guilt of being undocumented. Fear of dealing with law enforcement. Isn't this kind of a tired story? Illegal Mexican man kills and robs white American, then does a runner?"

"I admit it's an easy sell. But I have to go where the evidence takes me," Bart said. "And the powers that be like simple stories and quick solves. Which so far means Santiago."

"And he didn't steal anything?"

A big sigh came out of my phone. "Okay, look, our

theory is Santiago left, put on the hoodie, returned to rob the place expecting no one would be there, got surprised by the victim, killed him, panicked, and took off. We got him on camera reentering the building."

"You got a fuzzy image of someone reentering the building. And his work log shows him at another job during the time the mystery person was there."

"Well, well. Maybe there's still hope for you as a PI. Thing is, the place he was supposed to be at has no security coverage of the doors. He could have logged in but actually gotten there later. And it's just a few minutes away."

One less thing for Ricky to do. "If he was going to steal stuff, how would he carry it?"

"Maybe he was after small stuff he'd cased. Maybe he planned to make a few trips back and forth. Maybe he had an accomplice in the vehicle. Maybe he's a moron. Who knows?"

"And maybe he didn't recognize a $15,000 watch," I said, with just an undertone of snide. But I got it. Bart was under pressure to move on to other cases. Which he did not particularly appreciate. Thus, his sub rosa assistance.

"Say, did I tell you about the new letter opener I got?"

* * *

Unmasked

Mary Jo Hart called. She was forwarding me the security footage and photos I'd asked for. While I had her on the phone, I got the new address she had for Amanda Aparicio.

It turned out to be a condo in a new Baron Regal Resort in Aspen. Among the upscale building's amenities were an indoor pool and spa, as Melanie had mentioned. Similar units were selling for prices that would make a Silicon Valley real estate agent blush. However, an online search of county records revealed that she had paid well below market price.

The good deals for Amanda Aparicio that flowed from Steve Stanhope's murder just kept coming.

I took a flyer and called the resort's administrative number. I said I was an investigator working on the Amanda Aparicio accident and was looking for some information about the recent decedent, one of their condo owners. Throwing in cop words like decedent often helped, as did forgetting to mention the private thing.

I was soon connected to a woman who said she knew who Ms. Aparicio was, or rather had been. She expressed dismay at the accident and death—it was clearly not new information—and asked how she could help.

"I was wondering if you had a record of who her employer was." It was worth a shot.

There was a pause, then, "Ms. Aparicio was about to

start working here."

Bingo! "In what capacity?"

"I'm afraid you'll have to talk to Mr. Chang, our general manager, for any more information."

But, no surprise, Mr. Chang was unavailable. She would give him my message. I asked her to mention that we could do this in person. Sometimes, that intimidates people, gets them to talk to me.

It seems this was one of those times.

Chapter 24

The man calling himself George Chang called. He sounded nervous as he said he was general manager for Baron Regal Resort. I later verified that he was indeed that George Chang, but as a trained detective I take no one at face value. Usually. And gotten burned at times when I haven't.

Chang pinned me down on who exactly I was, and his tone changed noticeably when he found out I was not a cop. He said that Amanda had been hired as his executive assistant. "We got a new investor who recommended her," he said without enthusiasm. Continuing in a flat voice, he added almost as an afterthought, "It's a terrible thing that happened to her."

If Chang knew anything else about Amanda Aparicio or her so-called accident, he wasn't about to share with me. And I had no leverage.

Once off the phone, I searched around and came up with a report on a financial website about the new investor Chang had mentioned. It seems that the lead investor in the resort had been Victor Ostrovsky, the deceased billionaire owner of Ostrovsky Manufacturing. He had died around the time the pandemic had started. Coincidentally, Ostrovsky had owned the yacht *Sweetwater* which not long afterward played a major role in a case of mine that became known as the *Sweetwater* Showdown in which I almost got killed.

All the report said was that Ostrovsky's share had been bought from his estate by Garrett Manfort. The same Garrett Manfort, it turned out, whose venture capital firm was behind Aztound Technologies.

Garrett Manfort had landed Amanda Aparicio a sweet new job along with a sweet deal on a luxury condo. Along with her sweet separation deal from Aztound Technologies. Too bad she hadn't lived to enjoy all that sweetness.

Amanda must have been a hell of an executive assistant.

* * *

I called Nick Marchetti. He called me back an hour later. "I'm pretty jammed Joe," he said by way of greeting.

"This should be quick. It's about the Stanhope case. Long story, but I'll keep it short. Turns out Garrett Manfort bought Victor Ostrovsky's share of an Aspen sky resort about the same time you were buying *Sweetwater*. Anything you can think of I should know about how those guys are connected?"

"Two hard-ass rich guys who were neighbors and drinking buddies before Victor died. Ostrovsky's widow wanted to turn assets into cash as quickly as possible and turned to people she knew to help with that. Like me and Garrett."

"Anything hinky about their relationship?" I loved using that Steph Curry word, made me feel like a hip Bay Area dude.

"Other than that they saw the world through the same lens and could be royal assholes to those they considered to be lesser mortals, nothing that I know of."

"Thanks."

We ended the call. I knew Nick would call if anything relevant popped into his head. And, as usual, he had not asked for any details. He knew I'd share them if and when it was appropriate. And if I didn't, it was okay with him.

I reminded myself that Maddie Stanhope was my client, and my mission was to find out who killed her husband. Then I reminded myself that Maddie was actually Ed Wax's client, and I was working on the case for Ed. I decided that my next move ought to be cleared with him.

Amanda Aparicio had been my prime suspect. Unless there was some smoking gun Bart Taylor was keeping secret, Javier Santiago was just a convenient scapegoat. Amanda's death complicated the picture unless it turned out to really have been an accident. But what were the odds?

So I called Ed. When he returned my call, I laid it out for him. My main concern was, could this hurt our client?

Ed agreed with my take on it. If, despite what she had told me, Maddie thought Amanda had been romantically involved with her husband or played some role in his murder, she might have sought vengeance. Without telling her lawyer and PI about it, as clients were wont to do.

"You're making good faith use of the police to help get the truth for our client. We can't help it if our client lies or isn't forthcoming. Got to assume she's innocent of wrongdoing. So go for it."

I called Bart Taylor. "I have some information the Colorado police may not have turned up that may help their investigation," I said. "It's about how Aztound Technologies and Baron Regal Resort are connected."

Why not let the Colorado cops investigate it for us? I figured they would take the lead better coming from another cop than a PI. And Bart would be even more likely to share information with me in the future.

I call it investigation by proxy.

Chapter 25

Ricky called. "I just left the house where Javier Santiago was supposedly living. But all I got was the old *'no entiendo, no hablo ingles'* runaround. I'm sure they know something, but no one would talk to me. Including neighbors."

"I should have seen that coming," I said. "How about I swing by and give them a try? Meanwhile, keep an eye out in case someone takes off."

"Roger that."

The house was in a tract of small ranch-style houses a few blocks east of Montague Expressway just north of 101. It was one of those neighborhoods struggling to hang on to lower middle class, with lots of mostly well-used cars parked everywhere.

I spotted Ricky. His car, like the man himself, was adept at blending into the surroundings. He gave no sign or recognition as I parked and walked up to the nicely maintained home with its barely landscaped but neat front yard. When I rang the bell, what sounded like at least two different dogs barked from inside. No one answered. I waited a good minute and rang again. Just one ring. And no impatient, heavy-handed knocking.

The dogs started up again instantly. I heard a woman's voice shushing them. When the door opened, a lady I instinctively wanted to call *abuela* eyed me with an icy stare.

In what I knew was good colloquial Spanish, I explained that I was a private detective not working for the police but for Steve Stanhope's wife, who had hired me to find out what really happened to her husband. "I know Javier is afraid of being accused of something he did not do," I said. "I just want to get to the truth."

I knew whoever lived in that house would know what I was talking about. I also knew that my Spanish would disarm them. It was learned growing up in a neighborhood where half my friends spoke Spanish at home and we kids were all bilingual and had no idea that was unusual until we were several grades into grammar school.

I was not invited inside. Nor were any of my questions answered, not even how she was related to Javier. But I was told that Javier was a good man, but he was afraid. She also wished me success in finding the real killer so Javier could return home to his family. Her last words to me were, "Javier knows nothing that could help you. I only wish he did."

I did not try to talk to the neighbors. If I ever needed

more from Santiago's family, that move would be counterproductive.

Ricky called two hours later. The only action at the house had been the woman I spoke to walking to the nearby grammar school with a toddler in a stroller and returning with a little boy in tow.

"I think that's enough surveillance, Ricky. I'd like a fresh set of eyes to review the case file."

"On my way," Ricky said.

Chapter 26

The reason Roxie loved Aztound was that they left her alone.

She had spent her entire life trying to get people to leave her alone and let her do her own thing. Growing up in South Carolina, her family came to realize early on that socializing was not one of those things. It wasn't that Roxie was shy, it was that she had her own interests, and they rarely included other people.

Left alone, she did fine in school, and she learned how to avoid attention, including the inevitable attempts at bullying. How do you bully a girl who just doesn't care? Those that tried quickly found less challenging marks.

College was even easier. She went to Duke on scholarship. It was a sprawling university where no one paid any attention to the brainy math major. Her parents were relieved to have her out of their home, and she found living alone delightful.

What Roxie was interested in was mathematics. The more arcane, it seemed, the better. She belonged to

Unmasked

several online communities of people with similar interests. People of all ages, from all over the world, who were anonymous except for their usernames. Though to Roxie they had rich personalities she discovered from their online postings and exchanges, often in the form of equations, proofs, logic arguments and clever computer code.

This was Roxie's world. All else, the so-called real world, was a means to enable her to spend time in her world. The real world was full of barriers to doing that, and she had spent her life learning how to avoid or overcome such obstacles.

* * *

After Roxie completed her PhD, she was recruited by various firms from Wall Street to Silicon Valley that were on the hunt for math geniuses. She briefly considered academia but was uninterested in either teaching or publishing, both of which unavoidably came with the opportunity to continue her research.

She took a job as a rocket scientist—a quantitative analyst—for a hedge fund based in Charlotte, North Carolina, working on mathematical models for sophisticated investment strategies. She was good at it and well paid, but she found the people she had to deal with way too intense and the hours the job required left little time for her personal pursuits.

Roxie had often overheard her mom, an accounts payable clerk, complaining about how she was left alone to do her job in obscurity. After several years as a quant, Roxie decided to try following in her mother's footsteps.

She headed 3,000 miles west to Silicon Valley, in part for the climate—both the weather and liberal culture were appealing—but also to put distance between herself and her old life. Unlike most making this migration, she did not seek to become a highly paid engineer or data scientist; her financial needs were modest. Instead, Roxie scrubbed her resume. Gone was the doctorate, leaving just a bachelor's degree in math. Gone was the quantitative scientist job title, replaced by the modest accounting associate. She applied for a position as an accounts payable clerk at a startup named Aztound Technologies and was hired. In no time, she was an expert at the job, especially when she realized she could get the automated system to do nearly all the work.

Roxie soon came to appreciate the accounting system, not only for its functionality but its built-in security and safeguards. But she realized that, despite these state-of-the-art features, like any system used by humans it was vulnerable to their misuse. And as so often happens, the worst user was the CEO. Chet Khatri mindlessly approved invoices for payment. Worse, he had Roxie help his consultants set up their payment accounts. This was an egregious violation of accounting separation of duties. You just don't let the accounts payable clerk set up the accounts to be paid that way, it invited bogus customer accounts and was an invitation to fraud. After discovering other such vulnerabilities, Roxie decided she had to protect the company from itself and silently set about putting her own safeguards in place.

That was six years ago. No one ever suspected that behind her humble accounting clerk mask there was a silent sentry, patrolling and protecting the company's financial system. She even used a cute little piece of spyware she got from one of her mathlete friends that grabs control of a computer's camera to keep an eye on things.

Since then, she had been left alone in blissful isolation. And she was free to pursue her math interests, often on her office computer in parallel to doing her incredibly easy job.

It was a freedom Roxie would fight to keep. And she understood it was now in danger. Because the IPO was essential to Aztound surviving as an independent company. No IPO meant the company would be a takeover target. Which could only be bad for someone in accounting, which always got swallowed up by the company doing the acquisition, a victim of the quest for synergy, a euphemism for cuts.

Now the IPO was threatened by the brouhaha over Steve Stanhope's murder. And Roxy was determined to quash that threat. It was something she was confident she could accomplish, but she had to maneuver carefully, because she was in uncharted territory, and she sensed risks lurking everywhere.

Roxie once more turned to her plant to help her think things through. It was a good listener.

Chapter 27

Detective Bart Taylor arrived in my office the next morning, once more with donut bag in hand. He got a couple of sodas out of the fridge, handed me my Diet Coke, pointed to the bag and said, "You get first pick."

I selected a Boston Cream. "Finally he treats me in the manner I deserve."

"Don't get too used to it. But, yeah, this time you deserve a treat."

"Because?"

"Got me brownie points with the Colorado cops and my brass."

Bart rooted around in the bag and came out with a cinnamon twist. "Your tip panned out. Seems the GM of the resort had been skimming construction and maintenance contracts using his brother-in-law's company. He figured that guy Manfort was sending Aparicio to spy on him. He and the brother-in-law decided to send Manfort a butt-out message. Brother-in-law ran Aparicio off the road with one of his big trucks. Those cops are probably still high-fiving their quick solve."

We toasted with our cans. "I'll bet you took credit for the tip," I said.

"Of course I did. Had to protect my source. But that's not what got me kudos from my bosses."

I didn't mind Bart drawing this out. Not while there were more donuts in that bag, which I demonstrated by finishing my Boston Cream and starting on a classic old fashioned. Bart, who was falling behind because he was doing all the talking, went on, "No, I'm riding high with the brass because solving Amanda Aparicio's murder unmuddied the water. Javier Santiago's still their guy."

"Their?"

Bart gave me a serious face and shrugged. "What can I do? I just investigate and follow orders. The arrest warrant for Santiago pretty much ended my involvement in the case, even though we went through the motions of digging around some more."

I could tell this made Bart uncomfortable, even though it was out of his control. Which was why he had been helping me, starting with the letter opener clues. I changed the subject.

"You think the Warriors will ever make the playoffs again?"

* * *

Bart left the bag behind this time. Not long afterward,

Unmasked

Sally arrived and volunteered unbidden to help me with the donut burden. "Don't want these to go stale," she explained as she grabbed herself a soda and took the guest chair.

I filled Sally in on Bart's news while she happily started on a chocolate glazed. So predictable.

"You're saying Amanda's murder wasn't connected to Steve's after all."

"That's the way it looks. Which puts her back as my number one suspect."

"Based on?"

"Based on trying to convince me she and Maddie were pals." I explained the subterfuge about Mandy and Maddie being giggling buddies. "She threw in the nonsense about Aspen-Austin and Melanie's place just to throw me off in case I became suspicious." I backtracked and explained that part as well. "She had a reputation as a prankster."

"So you think she was trying to deflect suspicion?" Sally said.

"Subtly, yeah. Sort of planting a seed along with the confusion," I said.

"But didn't you tell me your client said she hardly knew Amanda and rarely spoke to her?"

"Exactly. Look, I'm not saying it was an effective ploy, but that doesn't mean she didn't try it."

Sally shook her head. "Some actual evidence might help. Anyway, if she did it, she's not talking."

"Cute. But here's something Ricky pointed out to me. He was reviewing the case file and noticed that Amanda's husband had been a butcher. Maybe she learned how to stick a knife between back ribs from him."

"That's not exactly hard evidence, Joe."

"I know," I said, "but Maddie deserves the truth and Javier Santiago deserves a fair deal."

"And you won't rest easy until that happens," Sally said.

Chapter 28

The first thing Garrett Manfort had done when the COVID lockdown was first announced in March of 2020 was call Chet Khatri. He had two messages for Aztound's CEO.

"Seize this opportunity," he commanded, his voice resounding with excitement. "We can shed a lot of the expense of office space. Permanently. That'll go right to the bottom line. So get this one right."

He told Khatri to get the best technology available for facilitating and monitoring work-from-home. Emphasis on monitoring. Subtext: control.

It was classic Manfort. A high concept, simple directive. Leave it to management to deal with all the messy details.

Manfort then made it clear this vision did not apply to all the staff.

"The company must see its leadership at the helm. You know, Captain Kirk on the bridge of the *Enterprise*." He chuckled at his waggish analogy. "You get that, right? Our enterprise needs a physical location and a leader with a steady hand. Surrounded by his crack team. That's especially important in times like these."

In truth, Manfort did not believe any such thing. He simply wanted his CEO where he could keep tabs on him. Keep control. Which was left unsaid. What was said was that he expected Khatri to keep working from his office at company headquarters. Pandemic be damned.

Chet Khatri appealed to Greg Culpepper, but the VC was careful to pick his fights with his fellow board member, and this was not going to be one of them.

Manfort then called Steve Stanhope. He told him about what he called Chet Khatri's plan to show great crisis leadership. And made certain his special protégé knew that he too would work at company headquarters where he could keep his eye on his CEO. Pandemic be damned.

Manfort did not stop there. Because if one special protégé in a company was good, two were even better. So it was that he had added Amanda Aparicio to his stable long before she and Steve Stanhope came to Aztound. Her assignment back then was to keep tabs for him on Stanhope himself. When Aztound started, Manfort not only seeded it with Stanhope as CFO, he also made sure that Khatri hired Aparicio as executive secretary for the two top executives.

Manfort informed Aparicio that he was counting on

her to work at the office during the lockdown, loyally and bravely supporting her CEO and CFO. Pandemic be damned.

Not to be shown up, and because he liked being at work lots more than staying in his lonely condo, Controller Howard Penning joined the pandemic-be-damned cadre.

As did Roxie Roxbury. When she learned about Khatri and the crew's plan to defy the lockdown, she decided that to protect her company she had to protect those fools from themselves.

Roxie discussed this with Mary Jo Hart, but though the office manager agreed that the others were acting recklessly, her overriding concern was protecting the wellbeing of herself and her family, particularly considering her age which put her at increased risk. Hart was going to scrupulously observe the lockdown.

Although no one had asked her to come to the office, neither did anyone try to stop her. Roxie came to work every day, assuring that each of the crew had a fresh N95 mask and a supply of wipes, disposable gloves, and hand sanitizer, and keeping a watchful eye on them with regard to the use of these measures as well as social distancing, all the while exercising extreme care for herself.

Not once did anyone in government check on why these cars showed up in the parking lot every day. No official so much as uttered a peep about Aztound Technologies' blatant violation of pandemic lockdown orders. And, remarkably, the seemingly gallant albeit foolish five remained virus-free.

Chapter 29

Ed Wax's office, again around the conference table.

The timestamp on the video displayed on the big screen reads 10:24 p.m. It shows Steve Stanhope unmasked, working at his desk. He looks up and says, "What are you doing here?"

A woman's voice. "Please talk to me."

"I told you there's nothing more to say. It's over."

A figure in a hoodie, wearing a mask, appears behind Steve. She removes the hood and stuffs the mask in the front pocket. She wraps her arms affectionately around Steve's shoulders.

"Stop that," he says, shaking her off. "You need to leave." His expression becomes one of puzzlement, perhaps because he notices, as do we, that she is wearing what appear to be disposable gloves.

For a moment, the video blurs. When it refocuses, we see Steve jerk forward, then attempt to rise. Still positioned behind him, the woman leans over, hands on his shoulders, her weight holding him down, her expression one of steely determination. Steve's face is a mask of abject horror as his head slowly falls face down.

*　*　*

"That's enough," Maddie said, as tears leaked down her cheeks.

I pressed escape to exit the video player, Amanda Aparicio's murderous visage indelibly etched in my brain.

Chapter 30

Tucked away in her cubicle, aided by her spyware, Roxie had become aware of the affair pretty much from the start, shortly after the lockdown commenced. She also saw it end.

She noted that Steve and Amanda tried to be discreet. Which should have been easy what with Chet holed up in his office and oblivious Howie being, well, oblivious. Their mistake was assuming that Roxie was oblivious as well. It was a guise she had long cultivated; it helped her learn so much about what people were up to. And they had no idea she was watching.

The new lovers had previously been friendly but proper colleagues, but the looks, touches, whispered conversations, and such were a dead giveaway that their relationship had become intimate. And continued long after things reopened.

Not that Roxie cared, other than about the COVID infection risk the two were taking. Until, that is, her beloved company was threatened.

Phil Bookman

* * *

After Amanda Aparicio's death, Roxie mailed a USB stick with the recording of Amanda murdering Steve to Joe Brink. Unlike the police, who seemed zeroed in on that poor janitor, Brink was out to find the truth for Steve's wife. That's what Mary Joe had told her, and Mary Jo was a good judge of people. Roxie trusted that Brink and the lawyer he worked for would see to it that the evidence was used properly. If not, she would take further steps.

That had not been necessary. The story of a woman scorned, however murderous, got mixed up with that same woman's murder in Colorado, and the Aztound Technologies angle was downplayed. The little soap opera had its fifteen minutes of fame, then faded away. Now a new, quite capable CFO was in place and Roxie felt certain the IPO was back on track.

It was too bad that she'd had to remove the spyware and erase its traces, but it was prudent to err on the side of caution. If they had known what to look for, the cops would have found it on Steve's laptop, but with the murderer already dead, the provenance of the video had garnered only cursory police investigation.

In no time at all, things were back to normal for Roxie and her faithful plant.

Acknowledgements

An author is just a writer without a good editor. I have been blessed with two. My wife, Lois Bookman, patiently makes sure my plots and characters hang together. My sister-in-law, Judy Reed, catches all the grammar, punctuation, and usage mistakes my word processor misses. Lois and Judy are also my cheerleaders, another requirement of my craft. I utterly depend on them.

I also want to thank readers who take the time to write a review on Amazon. I love the feedback, and others appreciate your thoughts.

* * *

This book is dedicated to the late Ron Oremland. I knew Ron for over 50 years, since we were college fraternity brothers. In addition to being a great friend, he was an author's dream reader. During our lunchtime conversations over Big *Fressers* at Max's Deli, Ron would frequently mention some of my characters as if they were mutual acquaintances. A brilliant scientist who was as much at home in the field as in the lab, Ron's oral tales of his adventures contributed ideas for several of my plotlines, though sometimes neither of us was aware of it except in retrospect.

Ron had a unique sense of humor and perspective on life, which he memorialized just before he passed in his memoir, *It was a Stark and Dormy Night,* available on Amazon. I highly recommend it.

About the Author

Phil Bookman, retired Silicon Valley tech entrepreneur, is the author of the Mike Gold Mystery Series and the Joe Brink Mystery Series. For more about Phil and his books, please visit his website at philbookman.com.

Contact Phil at philtheauthor@outlook.com
Visit Phil's author page at philbookman.com
All Phil's books are available on Amazon.com

Also by Phil Bookman

Fiction
Joe Brink Mystery Series
Venture Capital Pie
Final Part
Rainmaker's Revenge
Manning Cross
Abandoned
Sweetwater

Mike Gold Mystery Series
Opium
Charisma
Riding the Tiger
Slice
Alias
Death Order
Gold Jihad
The Yippee Murders
Gold Moonshot
Santa's Village
Wind and Fire
The GLEE Trilogy

Non-Fiction
Attacking The Crown Jewels

Made in the USA
Middletown, DE
07 November 2023